The Line in the Sand

Antonio Arch

Published by Antonio Arch, 2023.

THE LINE IN THE SAND

First edition. October 22, 2023.

Copyright © 2023 Antonio Arch.

ISBN: 979-8223763376

Written by Antonio Arch.

Dedicated to the memory of Margaret Bodden Arch

Prologue

"I'm too pretty to go to prison."

"I'm too pretty to work this hard."

"Suh hep muh crise, the next one o' you to open yuh mout' won't need to worry 'bout yuh looks." The silence lasts longer this time; perhaps nearly as long as a minute.

Near the civilised, growing community of Savannah sits the stately, sole remaining relic from a long-ago era in the history of the Cayman Islands. Pedro St. James is steeped in stories. Some of them are true, and others the stuff of legend. Nobody would believe what this carload of upstanding citizens is about to do, even those of us who believe the swashbuckling legends. And if they don't get caught, that is. The house and grounds are at their most hauntingly beautiful at night, but the national historic site is seldom visited at this ungodly hour when a black Land Rover pulls into the parking lot.

"You mean to tell me they leave all those lights on all night?" asks a passenger in the back seat.

"They don't see the bill. You think they gon' worry about them lights if none of them pay the bill?" replies the driver of the large car with another question. "Now remember what we agreed. Nobody talks once we get out. And pray there ain't no night watchman."

"I'm not saying a word. Not a damned word," says passenger number three as he points to the precious cargo in the back of his beloved SUV. "And we don't need to worry about him. He won't be sitting up to call for more champagne or a chilled glass."

There are in fact four passengers in the Land Rover. Three of them are nervous, animated, and sweating profusely before they even leave its air-cooled comfort to begin the last leg of their unpleasant journey and mission. The fourth neither speaks nor sweats for once in his life. He is quite dead and has been lovingly rolled up and sealed in the very area rug that he died on a short while ago. The ends of the rug are done up with heavy-duty tape the whole parcel has been bound with rope for easy carrying.

"If only you two knew how much this rug cost. My mother had them custom-made. In Iran, if memory serves me." The lament is ignored. It's too damn hot.

Even late at night, the weather in Cayman can feel so harsh that just getting out of the car for the short walk to a door (or in this case, the cliffs and ocean) can seem like a life decision. Relative humidity can remain at an uncomfortable dew point for so long that a thunderstorm becomes a welcome break. Tonight, while hot and humid, is clear and a breeze churns the waves over some of the deepest waters on earth, waters that will hopefully be their salvation in helping their rolled-up delivery get lost forever. If only the party can get it from car to water without breaking a toe or a heel.

"And I just had a manicure," wails the living, breathing male in the party.

"Yeah, me too,"

"Will the two o' you hush up? What the hell did I just say?"

"Sorry. Sorry," declares the man, who then decides to add another apology. "Sorry. We'll get you a manicure when this is all over."

"I never had no manicure. Not in my whole damn life."

"Never had a manicure? Please tell me the same isn't true for your feet. Those cloven hooves of yours deserve some TLC."

"Unnah leave my poor feet outta this. Watch it or you gon' drop him on his head."

"Have you never had a spa day? I'm gonna get you a gift certificate. Or maybe we should all go together. I'll call Ramona – "

"Which part o' the word silence the two o' you don' understand?"

Ironshore really can be very treacherous and unforgiving. They have all climbed along the ancient volcanic rock in their youth to explore the tiny wildlife left behind in rock pools by retreating tides. Decades of office work and orthopaedic shoes mean that their feet are as unprepared for this mission as their hands. They are forced to put down the handwoven rug several times to rest and switch positions before getting to the edge of the cliff. They carry out the task of swinging and flinging the cargo into the ocean with a surprising lack of fanfare.

"Does anyone want to say something? Poetry? A little something from the bible? Or we could sing something, maybe. I could start us off on *Shall We Gather By the River*?"

"Start us off or get us caught?"

"Sing the Jewel Song from Faust, for all I care. I'll be in the car."

"I need a cigarette. And we need to get the hell outta here."

The rug and its contents resist sinking at first, but the weights taped to the body eventually overpower any pockets of air, and they wait another thirty seconds to make sure that it does not resurface a fourth time.

"Sonafabitch was beginnin' to remind me of a Clive Cusslah novel."

"Well, that went well. Don't you think that went really well?"

"And look at us. Taking team building to a new level. I really wish this could go on our annual reviews."

"Well I wouldn't know about well. Seeing as how I never done nothin' like that before."

And it has not gone well. Not by any yardstick can the disposal of the body been measured to go well. For these three, who just a few short hours ago did not think that they could get away with disposing of the body of their victim, have in that time gotten far too confident since leaving the electoral district of West Bay. Not once since leaving those red lights at Eastern Avenue have they looked behind them because they were far too worried about the prospect of getting found out at Pedro St. James. It never once has occurred to these three accomplices that they might have been followed at a distance, almost from their point of origin at Seven Mile Beach. But they have been observed and now were just photographed by the pressing of a perfectly-manicured and expensively moisturized index finger. That finger belongs to a master criminal more dangerous than the idiot trussed in the rug and far more diabolical than these three friends could ever imagine.

1.

"You'll be lucky to get a room in the hotel, a place at dinner or even a stool along the bar during high season at this gem of a hotel. But it's worth it. There are bigger, showier hotels along the beach, bigger pools and flashier restaurants, complete with hipster chefs. But this place is quiet, elegant, comfortable and they know how to spoil their guests."
–HughandDianeB, UK

From a distance, the Corniche Hotel is dwarfed by her neighbours like a plastic piece on a board game. She holds her own at the north end of the beach, near the town of West Bay. She has been sitting there defiantly, longer than all her competitors, on real estate that could yield her owners tens of millions of dollars each. Developers have come from all over to approach her custodians about redeveloping the site, partnering up or selling the site.

"Knock it down, excavate a parking garage and build ten stories," they tell the board members of the Corniche Hotel Trust Ltd. But people like that should never get to touch a grand-dame like the Corniche.

Some of these developers purchased nearby parcels over the past few decades, then pulled down the buildings and built something much more significant, usually higher and mid-century modern. The Corniche seems tiny compared to the monstrosities that have been built on the neighbouring parcels of land. She was built in an era when local law stated that the top of any building could not be taller than the peaks of the nearby palm trees. Until the planning laws were amended in the 1990s, this meant that no structure had more than a few stories. So squat and low she will likely remain, until the day when it's finally decided she is to be rebuilt.

It was 5 am, and most of her inhabitants fast asleep. The sleeping guests might eventually stumble downstairs to the dining room for breakfast. Juice (blood orange, cranberry and pomegranate) and croissants, bagels and muffins under a silver dome are always set out on a tray at the poolside Champagne bar for the early swimmers and lovers of sunrise beach walks. Some of the guests were already beginning to stir, and to think about going down to the beach before it got too crowded and hot. Others would emerge much later, in their sunglasses and straw hats, smelling of coconut oil and hangovers, in search of a restorative Bloody Mary. The other essential staff of the hotel were just beginning to arrive, one or two as hung-over as the guests sleeping it off upstairs.

A decrepit white car pulled ever so slowly into the parking lot. The large freight-laden truck behind it swerved into the centre turning lane, speeding up to 50 miles per hour. The driver oblivious of yet another new roundabout just around the next bend. He had also forgotten that the speed limit along Seven Mile Beach has been 25 for years now.

"Drive on, fool. Drive on," said the driver of the car. "Hell ain't half full." She shot a hateful look to the north, through a window opened to enjoy the early morning air. The driver of the freight truck leaned on his horn. "Not a goddammed drop o' brought-upsy either."

The woman parked in an empty spot, got out of her dilapidated old jalopy, and looked up at the sky. She had seen this view of it thousands of times in her life and considered it her patrimony. As the land was getting so expensive, the last part of her lovely island that she could afford was this view. But she knew better. It was still hers, even if it's just a few grains of sand that she might call her own. "No time feh philosophy," she told herself.

She leaned against the car, worrying that h r slight weight might actually damage it while taking a minute to enjoy her breakfast menthol. Her middle-aged face was lined, but firm and her eyes kind despite the things they'd seen. They looked up and immediately darkened. Someone else might gaze fondly at the flat calm that Seven Mile Beach offers early in the morning. She didn't need a TV channel or the internet to tell her that some sort of storm was brewing.

"Suh hep muh Crise," said Lorna Paige Ebanks as she exhaled the smoke.

*

"God!" remarked Oren Goldberg as he stepped out and onto the balcony of Penthouse 4 to catch the sunset. The sunset had in fact caught him off guard instead. Try as he might, Oren could never quite describe or explain what it was about a Caymanian sunset that would convince visitors, bankers, seafarers and generational Caymanians to stop, look up and be thankful.

There had been articles in science journals that attempted to explain the visual effect, but even those written for the layman made no sense to Oren. All he knew for sure was that this was indeed a million-dollar view, and they were lucky to have two suites to rent which faced onto the sunset. At two thousand dollars per night they were a steal. Well, they would be a steal if they were occupied.

"Whah happen now?" asked the voice on the other end on the phone at his ear. "Hit yuh toe on that door track again?"

He couldn't imagine why the suites were unoccupied. The Corniche had been built in the Regency Moderne style in the 1960s by his late parents. Some of the big new chain hotels that towered over it had not weathered even a decade of hurricane seasons. They had been built with foam, drywall, prefabricated modules and pods. Their owners could boast of improvements in energy efficiency, but they couldn't boast of the sturdy, enduring strength of poured, reinforced concrete.

"No, no. I'm fine. Just looking at the sunset. First time today I've looked outward and thought of the beauty around us."

Even the interior walls were solidly clad, which made renovations and upgrades difficult and costly, but she was always the first hotel on the island to be back in service when the occasional hurricane visited the island. She was heavyset with travertine, terracotta tiles, mahogany and brass. Some of the online reviews said she was more akin to a private gentlemen's club than a boutique hotel on the beach, and her guests never went anywhere else. One British gentleman had been coming every winter for the past twenty years and had the same penthouse suite booked in advance for his next ten winter holidays. He was on a first-name basis with Oren and certain members of his staff ; they met up every so often for cards, dominoes, cigars and copious amounts of hotel brandy.

"Yuh daddy would be so happy if he was here to know his money had been well spent on that philosophy degree, then."

"Don't be such a cynic, Lorna. Come join me for a Red Stripe when you get the day's dirt?"

"Soon come," was her sharp, efficient reply from downstairs.

Miss Lorna was the housekeeping manager at the Corniche. The antiques and art were authentic, the mattresses checked, flipped and aired with each arrival and the corners and crevices were cleaned whether they appeared dusty or not. She picked her products carefully; they always smelled either of lemons or lavender and never clashed. "Nothing goes together quite like lemons and lavender," she had once scolded a salesman who had tried to sell her a product line of commercial cleaners that didn't meet her nose's standards. "I use a dry cloth on Mr Goldberg Senior's antiques and a tiny spritz o' lemon oil when the wood needs care – never, ever anything else." She was the custodian of the hotel's interiors and had been in charge of linens, surfaces and that trademark smell for over two decades. She and Oren always used Mr and Miss. in front of one another's first names in the public areas, but had been eating at each other's homes and cheating each other at cards and dominoes since their youth. They saw eye to eye, and to everyone's surprise they held one another in awe and respect, despite their differences. She was almost due for her gold watch, two weeks of vacation and bonus to celebrate her quarter-century at the hotel. Not that she would ever wear a gold watch.

As custodian of the Corniche brand, Oren had no one above him to shake his hand and present him with one of his own. Like it or not, he was the president and his parents were both long gone. He liked to think that they were remembered daily in the details and design of the business that they left behind.

The four penthouses came with unlimited tea and canapés in the afternoon, cocktails before or after dinner on the balcony and their own dedicated valet. Lorna usually turned down the beds herself, inspecting and polishing each piece of fruit that went into the fruit bowl and dusting each and every light bulb before the guests arrived. Lorna had her own budget for everything and anything needed in these suites – French linen water and candles inspired by the surf and fresh air were employed throughout, with a lavender candle lit every evening around sundown in the hallway to signal the end of the day and promote relaxation.

The bars (never mini-bars as you might expect) were stocked with top-shelf liquor including a bottle of Courvoisier and four oversized snifters. There were four each of crystal-white wine, red wine, Champagne and liqueur glasses, all of the highest quality. Someone (usually Lorna) returned to the suites before every arrival to inspect, hand-polish and replace the glasses precisely an inch from one another, and an inch from the edge of the shelf in the bar cupboard. There was a split of Champagne in tiny refrigerators concealed beneath the counter behind polished mahogany doors, as well as whatever else was listed on the guest profile in the Corniche's CRM system. Once upon a time, they had kept guest preferences on a five-by-seven-inch index card in the downstairs office, but the staff had long ago retired these old guest files and now an email was circulated whenever they were expecting returning guests detailing their last stay, preferences and special requests. "Times sure change," Lorna was often heard to say when someone downstairs attempted to bring her and Oren up to speed on the latest technologies and trends.

Oren never grew tired of observing the chorus of people and checklists that made the place so much more than a building. He was particularly interested in the lives and idiosyncrasies of the staff who had been there the longest. Although he didn't exactly take an active part in the daily operation, no one could say that Oren didn't take a dedicated interest in the smooth running of his father's hotel. He was sure to miss this view if they ever lost it.

He loved this time of day. The early evening was his favourite period, and the balcony his preferred place for spending it. It offered a front-row seat to the legendary sunsets that Seven Mile Beach offered. The sky to the west had turned a combination of orange, pink and crimson, while a deep and dark purple was slowly creeping from the east to overtake and subdue the vibrant splash of colours. The daily show would be over soon.

He only just heard the treble of the assertive knock on the door of the room behind him, followed by a voice calling "Housekeepin'!" A moment later, a familiar face peeked in, and he beckoned her to enter. "I goin' soon. You need anythin' else? Soap? Turn-down? Shampoo?" She winked at the hotel's bald owner as he rose, removed two beers from the bar, pulled out a chair from the balcony table and placed an ashtray at the centre. The housekeeper crossed the sitting area of the bar and shut the balcony door behind her. She accepted the chair and groaned as she lowered herself into it.

"What-a-gwan?" he asked, doing his best impression of her Caymanian accent. Lorna took a long, grateful mouthful of beer then lit a menthol cigarette, pushing the pack across the table so that he could help himself. "I came up here to enjoy the sunset."

In spite of her cynicism, Lorna could still be distracted by the dramatic colours of the setting sun. But now she forced herself to drag her eyes from the sky, looked at her boss mischievously, smiled and shook her head.

"Nuh. You came up here to avoid all the crazy goin' on in the lobby. Yuh think I fool? I can't say I blame you. You know, Oren. I gotta worry about the state of the world. You remembah when what it was like in times past an' famous people behaved like famous people?"

"I know what you mean. So tell me. What's happened this time? More skinny-dipping? Champagne in the bathtub? Multiple room guests?"

"I remember when I first came here, one day I had to run some extra matches, or ashtrays or somethin' up to this here very suite. You know who was sitting over there?" Lorna took another grateful gulp of her favourite beverage before leaning forward and whispering the name of a movie star who they both adored and who had once stayed at the Corniche.

"I still have the note she left on her stationery. It was addressed by hand to *Miss Lorna*, and she thanked me for every bobby pin I brought up here, the cold cream for her sunburn and the ashtray and matches. I still got it framed at home. I was so young and felt so foo-foo I was 'fraid to talk to her. Best of all? Her eyes was honest-to-god violet. The prettiest eyes you evah looked into."

"Things have changed, haven't they?" Oren asked, knowing the answer.

"Yuh nuh tellin' me. We got people down there snappin' they fingers at us, asking us where they can score some ganja, or if we can send a girl up. You believe that? A girl. Like it was a bucket o' ice or somethin'. And that lil fool downstairs is bearin' down on my last nerve."

"You shouldn't talk about Sharon like that," he joked. "She's your cousin. And the manager."

"I ain't talkin' 'bout Sharon. But she in second place. That ass is due back tomorrow too. Pratt. A royal visit don't take as much work as him, and his six Louis Vee-tawn bags."

"Yeah, well I've got Mr Pratt figured out. I used to think that he worked as an informant for one of the tabloids, or was maybe a paparazzo himself. Turns out he's nothing near that glamorous."

"Well if he snaps his fingers at me one more time, he gon' find himself takin' pictures of the inside o' his bunkey." The housekeeper pulled on her menthol. "Things have really changed in this world. People nowadays comin' here behave like they come outta God-knows-where."

This was how the owner and the head of housekeeping spoke to one another whenever they found a private opportunity. Oren chuckled at her observations of the hotel, staff, guests and life in general. If the Corniche was a grand-dame, then Miss Lorna was her corset, and he was beyond content to know that after all these years they shared this private shorthand language. She was a perfectionist, this connoisseur of lemons and lavender. Everywhere had to smell clean and Miss Lorna had been ensuring that the Corniche sparkled as if it was the most important job ever bestowed on anyone. Every morning she did her rounds as the sun came up, studying, inspecting, scrutinizing everything from the waterline of the pool to the lobby washrooms – the bowls had to be fresh and the mirrors pristine, while the smell had to meet her trademark expectations and the fronds of the potted palms had to look happy to be there.

They peered over the balcony to find the source of a raised voice. A small child was pointing out to sea, describing a large marine animal, a killer whale or giant squid that had followed her to shore. Her parents were comforting her with wide open arms

"What that pickney makin' all that fuss for?"

"Oh, that big brain coral out there. The one where the school of fry live."

"Made me forget what I was...oh yeah...somethin' just ain't right about that lil man. I can't put my finger on what it is, but he's trouble. Every time you look his way he's up in somebody's business. Mark my words."

2.

"We always have such a great stay at the Corniche. You don't get comfort like this anymore. They just don't make hotels like it and I'm glad that year after year you can expect the same experience!!" –CByrne, Cayman Brac

"Pratt. Checking in." Nobody knew how to make an entrance like Mr Pratt. Sharon, like most of the staff at the Corniche, thought that, in his attempts to make a spectacle, he only succeeded in making an ass of himself. But in his own mind, he was doing something far more subtle and useful. He was making an entrance.

"Good afternoon, Mr Pratt. Welcome back to the Corniche." She kept her smile attractive but professional.

"Hello," he said, placing emphasis on the second syllable of the greeting, using his drama school mid-Atlantic diction. It seemed the girl was increasing the wattage of her smile. Maybe she wanted to jump his bones. You sly dog, Paul. You've still got it.

"Oh, dear. I'm so sorry for the delay Mr Pratt, but we weren't expecting you until after four."

"This is most inconvenient," he said, puffing up his chest. "I've been travelling all day." She contained the snort that threatened to come out of her nostrils – JFK to GCM hardly counted as all-day travel.

"Let me see what I can arrange for you, Mr Pratt," she said, wary of falling for one of his tricks yet again. There had never been a visit during which the man hadn't found something so heinous, so filthy, or so atypical of the Corniche that it hda warranted a room upgrade, complimentary bottle of Champagne or handwritten note.

14

"Surely there must be something. This is most unlike the Corniche," he continued, as if on cue. He looked to his left and right, assessing his audience and the cast of fellow players in the wings.

It was shaping up to be one of those days. And it was about to get worse.

Nobody liked a confrontation but there was just no avoiding them sometimes, especially working as closely as they all did. The next crisis began when Oren arrived far earlier than usual, more animated and asked for a meeting.

"Well. You two won't believe this."

Lorna could tell that Sharon's nose was out of joint and that she would spend the day like this. Sharon didn't seem to like it when Oren called meetings that included both of them. It must have something to do with rank. Lorna understood these things, of course. She knew that she hadn't been to college and university and didn't have any hotel training, but Oren was just saving himself from having to repeat himself later. If the problem involved hands getting dirty, knees getting bent or manual work, Sharon would just turn around and delegate anyway. But Sharon sure loved what she called the chain of command.

"This time Percy has gone too far," continued Oren.

"This about Percy?" asked Lorna. "This early?"

Percy was a legend, worthy of a human resources textbook. The only reason he still had a job at the Corniche was that they had all been covering for him. If he got fired, it was safe to say that nobody else in their right mind would ever hire him, as a concierge or anything else. Sharon had stopped adding entries to his file. She had stopped warning him. Everybody knew that there was no point. The man was a legend.

There was the time that Percy had been invited upstairs by guests to "party" in their room. When the party got out of hand hours later, Percy had been found asleep in the corner, in a sitting position, missing several pieces of clothing. This had saved his job. When questioned, Percy offered to swear on his family Bible that he remembered nothing and had likely been roofied before being kidnapped and molested. His storytelling skills had saved his career while cementing his reputation.

Less than a year later, Lorna began noticing bottles of powerful prescription painkillers in guest bathrooms with Percy's name on them. The maid found the concierge's excuses poetic, no downright-plain-haiku. "Pickpockets. Crick-neck."

Lorna had been confident that the Corniche's concierge would lose his job after the most recent holiday party when Oren had been drugged, probably by accident. This had happened minutes after Percy had returned from the bar with a tray of drinks. Oren had made the unfortunate mistake of choosing the same cocktail as a young intern who Percy had taken a shine to. Nothing could be proven in the madness that followed, but Lorna was no fool. The long drive from George Town and the emergency room to the Goldberg house, after he had submitted to having his stomach pumped, had allowed Lorna time to think and reconstruct everybody's movements at the party. It wasn't the first time that Oren had needed trussing to the passenger seat.

"I ain't sayin' it's him, Oren. I got no proof. But I can tell you one goddammed thing. It's a good thing...well, two good things. He won't be mixin' me no more drinks. And you's lucky it wasn't you Percy had designs on."

Today Oren was fit to be tied as he began to tell of his story of being out the previous evening. Seeing his fury, Lorna could hardly wait for the day's entertainment.

The owner of a nearby restaurant Oren had been visiting for years had seen Oren and approached him.

"Poor guy. He was apprehensive about even bringing it up. Something about snitches getting stitches. I still have no idea what that means."

"Whah happen now?" Lorna said, impatiently. Sharon was leaning forward too.

"Percy was there a few weeks ago for dinner and drinks. Sat at the bar and they took advantage of the opportunity to chat him up for more business, expecting to comp him for dinner that night. Now I could turn a blind eye to him accepting a night out every now and then."

"Oren, what happened?" asked Lorna again. Sharon nodded, for once thankful that her cousin could talk to the hotel owner like this.

"He demanded a monthly fee for referrals. And he didn't suggest it so there was no room for misinterpretation. He demanded."

Lorna and Sharon were amazed at the amount, which was more than Percy made at the Corniche on a busy week, including gratuities.

"Oh no. and if he's done it at one place, then he's probably done it at others." Said Sharon.

"Nice knowin' you, Percy," said Lorna. She knew before another word was said that this was the end of Percy's hospitality career. Sharon would endure a lot. She might even turn a blind eye to Oren being sedated and molested, but she would not allow the concierge to remain in light of this level of insubordination. "Who was you out for dinner with?"

"Oh, just some friends. You don't know them."

"You got friends that I don' know?" Oren became slightly but noticeably agitated to Lorna's eagle eye.

"Well of course I have friends that you don't know, Lorna. And vice versa I'm sure."

"Okay, Oren. If you say so. But it's more likely you was out lookin' somethin' else." They parted ways – Sharon to terminate Percy, Lorna to clean and polish and Oren to do whatever it was that Oren did.

***

"I can't stand that man. I just can't stand him," Sharon said to the group seated around the small back office table during a gossip break a short while later.

"I bet he doesn't know how annoying he is or he probably would've changed his name by now."

"You'd think someone might break the news to him. I mean, the man must have friends. Right?"

"I think that's a lot to ask of anyone..."

"To tell him that he's annoying?"

"No. To be his friend."

"Why does he sound like that every time he checks in?"

Most hotels prepare meals for their staff, especially lunch. It's usually an institutional mess, much like what gets served in prison. The Corniche had never prepared that kind of staff meal. They served a light lunch in the dining room, available between 10:15 and 11:15 before the doors opened for guests, and an after lunch (2:30 to 3:30). Depending on when a member of staff arrived, they could enjoy a gourmet meal in the dining room or one of the coveted club sandwiches that were sent out to staff too busy to leave their desks or posts. The gourmet poutine, Caesar salads with chicken breasts and grilled four-cheese sandwiches were of the same quality that was served to guests.

"I know the man talkin' English," said Lorna, "but all I can hear when he open his mouth is fluent jackass."

"He's so condescending. Pretentious. Ridiculous man." said Sharon. "Who does he think he is? An actor in an old black and white movie? And that collection of oversized sunglasses. God. They make his face look even tinier than it is. Every time."

"What?"

"You know what I mean!"

"I know exactly what you mean. Every time he makes that poppy-show entrance as if he's the Queen of Sheba. I just enjoy you trying to explain it to me without cussing."

"Don't you mean the King of Sheba?"

"No, queen. That man is a bona fide drama queen."

"Eediot."

"He certainly knows how to conduct the front of house like we're an orchestra specializing in waltzes."

"It takes a seasoned hospitality professional to deal with him. He's written the book of dirty tricks of getting free stuff in hotels. He's so much more than ice buckets and breakfast vouchers."

"I hear ya. We ain't talking playing cards. This man is the king of the room upgrade. He can waltz in here and go from a single berth to a suite like that." Sharon snapped her fingers for effect.

Bobby the bartender (and now acting concierge) appeared with his lunch, sitting down to join them during the lunchtime lull at the bar: "Seriously? How? I mean, I know the dude is slippery. But you mean he's that smart?"

"I don't know about smart, but he sure does know how to sniff out an opportunity. For example, the tactic that he pulled today. You show up to check in several hours before your room is supposed to be ready, throw a fuckin' BF and make it look like it's the hotel's fault."

"What's a BF, again?"

"A Bitch Fit. From *White Chicks*. You need to brush up on your hotel acronyms."

"He's never sober."

"Remember the first time? He showed up here with no reservation and pretended to cry because we'd lost his booking." Sharon shook her head.

"I remember that week. I remember it well. You think you had it bad downstairs? That jackass nearly died in his room." Lorna looked over at the others around the table.

"What? How?"

"By my own hand. Tha's how."

The room went silent, and all at the table seemed to lean towards her. Lorna hadn't planned on telling this story again, but this lot eating their lunch were so green that it could be her piece of community service for the day.

"We didn't know him at this point, not like we know him now. One day, I went up to deliver some extra towels and robes. And shampoo and soap. Some things never change, yunnuh. Even on his first visit, he needed a goddamned revolving door."

"Sounds like Pratt." Added Oren.

"Doesn't sound like a fond memory," said Bobby.

"Chile, you nuh heard the best part yet. So I lay the robes down on the bed, then the towels. I went to put the toiletries on the coffee table, but it already had a mound of white powder on it so big you'd think it was soap and he was washing his draws. And I realized when I looked up that he was practically on top of me. Not only that, but he was between me and the way out. The jackass. He made some ridiculous invitation to stay. Hang out. Like I didn't have better things to do than sit around watching him grind them horse-capped teeth.

"Oh, God."

"Don't worry. I got outta there, alright. I'm only telling this to remind all of you to be wary of people like that. I wanted to get out of the damn room without no fuss, but he was half-lit and decided to offer me a glass of Champagne and a line of whatever that was on the table. I told him I had never put nothin' up my nose. Or ever tasted Champagne."

"I bet that's when he got really... Pratt." Bobby looked visibly upset. Lorna reached over, squeezed his arm and gave him a faint smile; it wasn't her usual playful look, but something powerful enough to crinkle her eyes.

"You said it. I don't know why but that made him try even harder to get one or both in me. He said we should get together. And he was winking at me like it was a nervous tick." She had altered her accent to sound more like his. "He didn't sound so classy that day. Gone from high society to ghetto. And he moves fast, our Mr Pratt. He made up the space between us and he was breathing up my neck. Yeah, up not down. Even with the lifts in his shoes he barely came up to my chin. When he reached out he looked like a child tryin' to get something off the top shelf he wasn't allowed to touch."

"Jesus, Lorna." Sharon was upset by this. She was always conscious that housekeeping staff put themselves at risk every time they knocked on a room door. It was more upsetting that something like this had happened at the Corniche and that she was only now hearing about it. "Why didn't you tell me any of this?"

"Because of what happened next," said Lorna, with her trademark look of defiance returning to her face.

"I...I was all but healed from a lumpectomy, but I was still tender. In more than one way, maybe. Well, the truth is I hadn't planned to knock him out. I was wanting to swat his hand like you would do a fly. But when I hauled off and batted his hand off my breast, he went flying across the room like we was in one of them Bugs Bunny cartoons. He even sat up and shook his head like they do." She gave her own head a brisk shake to illustrate.

"Good. One bitch lick mighta taught him a lick o' sense," said Bobby.

"He got up, and all the charm was gone. He called me a dyke, a bitch, a half-breed. Threatened to get me fired. I got out my blue dust cloth and walked over to the powder on the table and said in my best maid voice, Oh I'm so sorry sir. I missed a spot, sir. But I gon' clean it up 'areckly, sir. That almost gave him his first of many coronaries."

"Did you wipe it up?"

"No. I told him if I ever had to so much look in his direction ever again, I would go down and tell this story to the management, my cousin the chief of police and my other cousin, who broke grown men's legs for a living."

"But Lorna, you nuh related to... " the room groaned.

"Did you ever tell anyone?"

"Long time had passed when I finally did. We always need guests to spend, and I thought he was flush with cash. Maybe he was in them days, for all I know. But to this day, the sight of me makes that vein on his forehead pop out." Lorna gave Oren a knowing smile.

"I didn't know you could handle a situation like that. Or fight off a man. Or make that sort of a management decision," said Sharon.

"Neither did I. Till that particular day."

The table clucked approval. "Lorna, you're a brave lady."

"Nah. That jackass is ninety pounds wet and four-foot-eleven without them wedges in his shoes."

***

Not far away, Mr Pratt was sitting in a lounger sunning himself in a speedo, gazing out at the kaleidoscopic sky and the Caribbean Ocean. He didn't really need the tan but had to do something while the girl tended to his suite. It had been a daunting party last night and he needed the TLC almost as desperately as his linens did. He had managed very little sleep.

It always amazed him how the cult of celebrity worked. The fact that he had appeared in a music video twenty-five years ago could still get him laid. No matter that it was one music video (making him a one-hit-wonder) followed by a terrible film and a sitcom that the network had pulled after only three episodes. It still meant that he was a celebrity, and he liked it. It didn't hurt that he still looked as good as he had when he had shot to notoriety. Of course, it cost time, money and some medical pain during the recovery process, but it was worth it. He still had it; his ease at hooking up last night had been proof...

He hoisted the flag on a pole attached to his lounge chair and waited an annoying five minutes for the server to come from the bar to take his order. He softened when his buddy Bobby trotted over. He liked Bobby. That boy was useful.

"And make sure it's cold this time, dammit. The only thing worse than Champagne that's warm or flat is cheap."

It was beginning to feel too quiet. Maybe he should have stayed at one of the larger resorts. Or one of the larger islands. This place was so small that there was no spa, and this little island so backwards that none of the employees or locals seemed to have heard of him. He wanted a reaction when he presented his platinum credit card – recognition, admiration, requests for autographs. But here all he got was the requisite printout. He couldn't even get free drinks here, and the girls from last night's session were island-hopping socialites, desperately on the hunt for bubbly, coke and sex.

His flute of vintage arrived, and the server waited while he made a big deal of closely examining the rising bubbles, holding it up to the light and tasting it to make sure it was vintage and a mere degree or two above freezing. He had seen this done in the movies.

"Very good," he said, waving the boy away. Sometimes you have to teach young people the value of carrying out a task properly. He liked things just so and the customer, as they say, is always right. He toasted the server's retreating back and took a long gulp to toast himself.

3.

"It doesn't get much better than the Corniche Hotel. They remember my name year after year. There are limited choices, but who needs choice when the best has been chosen for you?!" –The Boutroses, Toronto

It was nearly four in the afternoon when Miss Lorna was finally able to get into her dilapidated old car and make the long drive home to Newlands. The parking lot was so hot by this hour that the trip from the staff entrance to the car had her sweating.

"Suh hep muh Crise," she swore to herself as she lit a menthol before making her way south on the beach road. Every day it seemed as if she was getting away later and later. Every morning she arrived at the hotel before dawn to start her day and begin the arduous task of working down her checklist. Granted, there were two more girls under her who were a godsend, but neither of them had Miss Lorna's eye for dirt, nose for odour, or dedication to the work. "Nobody don't take no pride in they work, no more," she often complained to her fellow staff when she was required to go behind one of them to straighten a cushion, get down on her knees to properly clean a corner or remove the smudge from a mirror.

With the competition getting fiercer and the profit margins getting narrower, the pressure on her was so intense that this was only her second cigarette for the day. She had eaten lunch in five minutes while standing up in the back office.

There was only one back office; housekeeping shared one desk, security and bookkeeping another and the rest of the staff shared a third. Serving staff would often have to share a surface while they counted up their cash, and there were very few secrets kept. If someone screwed up, everyone knew about it. This could drive a perfectionist like Miss Lorna wild with rage. A lone, coarse hair on a newly made bed was still being thrown in her face years later. "Remember the time that fool girl made the bed with the pubic hair?"

Days like this annoyed Miss Lorna. Leaving at this time of day, she would be getting home even later because school was letting out. The school buses would be heading east at the same time, and she just wanted to overtake them, get home, put up her feet, light another menthol and open a beer. It had been an uneventful day, but she had kept herself busy, especially as the other part-time housekeeper had called in sick. These girls were getting more and more brazen with their truancy and less creative with their excuses. This morning's call had used menstrual cramps as an excuse.

"Unnah ready for this?" Miss Lorna had said when it was her turn to report at this morning's early-morning meeting. "Lucinda says she can't come today because she gettin' her period. Christ almighty..." Another team in another hotel might have laughed this off, but here at the Corniche, her colleagues all shook their heads in disbelief and sympathy with the day ahead for Miss Lorna. "Even when I was young enough to get mine I woulda sooner dead than call here and tell somebody that."

"But Lorna, you done gon' through the change yet, ain't you?" said one of the back office team playfully. The feigned concern got the desired laughter and covered mouths.

"You try so don' frig wid me today, woman. Or I gon' call the Labour Board. Your ass'll be grass, and I gon' be the lawnmower."

This was typical of the back office. Tasteless sparring and dirty jokes were what got the staff through the challenges of the front of house, where everyone smiled so much that it wasn't uncommon to complain of face-aches.

***

Traffic had slowed to 25 in the 40 zone she was driving through; at this speed she doubted that she would get home in time for *Jeopardy* and *Wheel of Fortune*. But Miss Lorna had another, more significant reason for getting home. She needed to check the shutters, the pantry and the expiration dates on the tins that she kept for reserves. Trouble don't blow shell, as the old people used to say, and trouble was closer than anyone realized. She had seen it in the sky this morning. Something was coming. A nor'wester? A storm? Worse? She wasn't as adept at these predictions as her mother's generation, but she knew that there was weather on the way.

She kissed her teeth in frustration as she looked over and saw the reminder shoved into the corner where the dashboard met the window. Halfway to Savannah, and now she had to turn around to get that parcel from the postal service that had been waiting to be picked up. She took advantage of a roundabout to make an about-turn and headed towards the parcel post facility near the foot of the runway. The package could have waited another night but she was curious. She ordered so many books and DVDs online that she had no idea what she was about to collect and take home.

The voluptuous woman at the end of the postal queue turned to nod at Lorna, who wasn't pleased to see someone she had been trying to avoid. "Lorna wah' yuh sayin'?"

"Not a thing, Linda-Lou. How's you?"

"Well let me tell you. Since the day I gave my heart to the Lord, I ain't needed so much as an aspirin, toothpaste or even a laxative."

"You didn't need to tell me that. I could see it on yuh face and lovely complexion. Yuh very countenance." Lorna pretended to hunt for something at the bottom of her bag, scared of an invitation to Linda-Lou's church of the month club to get saved and baptized. The number of times this woman had been immersed in the waters of Smith

Barcadere, Lorna would have thought she could go through her day looking a little cleaner and smelling somewhat fresher.

She picked up one romantic suspense set in a large country house, one light horror and almost seventy episodes of three of her favourite high-budget 1980s series, then she was finally on her way home to indulge and binge.

"This is my boss, Jonathan Hart," she said as she wished she had a Max waiting ahead of her with the table set with her dinner.

4.

"We've just returned from our stay at the Corniche. Everything is so perfect that I suspect they sift their sand and comb the beach! Every lettuce leaf, coaster and ice cube seem to be hand-picked!" –Lturner, Montreal

"Ladies and gentlemen, welcome to the Baham...uh...beg pardon. Welcome to the Grand Cayman Islands, ladies and gentlemen."

Sir Hugh hated to make a fuss, but it did seem to him that passengers who took this flight regularly would feel more at ease and comfortable if that voice got the place and the local time right. It might even undoubtedly restore his own long lost confidence in the airline. For the first half of the flight, the voice had kept referring to a Nassau that rhymed with "ass-hoe"; none of the passengers seemed to notice this any more than they had noticed the safety demonstration.

"I like to come prepared," the sunburned lady sitting next to him had said, shortly after they had boarded and been sealed into the ancient, slightly mouldy-smelling aircraft. She had wiped down her seat with an antiseptic wipe, offering him one. She showed him a plastic bag of snacks, magazines and bottled water. "You just never know."

"What do you suppose will go wrong this time?" he asked.

"Lunch," she answered with a deadpan face, knowing exactly what he meant. "Or the entertainment will break down, and all those students in the back will demand we turn around."

The flight was packed to the gills, and it was neither as smooth nor as pleasant as the welcoming, soothing voice had predicted upon departure. Their rough crossing across the Atlantic was thanks to the enormous weather system that had formed and was slowly creeping towards the low-pressure area that straddled the northwest Caribbean. It had already been gaining form, momentum and strength even while he had been studying the satellite images in the departure lounge and watching experts attempting to predict its path. He was reminded by a conversation in front of him in the queue in the arrivals hall that the system had been named already. Lisa.

But the flight had at least crossed the Atlantic without any mechanical incident, although the Boeing Triple-Seven didn't quite manage a soft touch down and after being trapped inside it for the past thirteen hours, a few passengers groaned as their backs and buttocks absorbed the shock. The runway was so hot that the heat was rising off the asphalt like a mirage. Everyone was eager to get down the stairs and make it into the terminal, but they were forced to sit at the end of the runway looking at the North Sound until airport employees were dispatched to shoo away a family of iguanas, who had been sunning themselves. They were known to make an unpleasant mess when they met with a wheel or the draft of a jet engine. His phone, which was now switched on after so many hours was repeatedly lighting up and chiming in protest at having been silenced for such an extended period. Most of the alerts were updates about Lisa.

"You come back so soon," the smiling taxi driver said as she helped him into his minibus. "You must love us like cook-food." Hugh had heard this amusing analogy often during his frequent visits to the island but had never quite figured it out. As opposed to raw food? He certainly loved this place a great deal. The driver grinned and shook his hand as if they were old friends, not as if she had merely driven Hugh to the hotel a dozen times over the years. "Where you goin', baby? Back to the Corniche?" She called him baby, babes, dahlin' or sweetheart too, which always made him smile, and think of the kindly housekeeper at the Corniche who always did the same. If he closed his eyes, he could hear her voice now: "If you needs anything, sweetheart. Anything at all, just call downstairs and ask for Lorna to run it up to you. You need yuh' coats and jackets sent out to clean? I don't suppose you'll need 'em here." Miss Lorna was more efficient than any valet.

Hugh had been coming to the Corniche for decades, and while the beach and surrounding landscape had changed dramatically, the hotel had not. The dining room downstairs could barely seat thirty, but it was striking, like a gentlemen's club or the smoking room on an ocean liner. The menus had barely changed either, and only to reflect best practices in conservation. The conch ceviche was replaced with lionfish when the season ended, and the turtle soup was a variation on the local recipe for stew, cooked in a base of yellow peppers and seasoned with local scotch bonnet. The turtle meat was farmed, of course, and sourced through legal channels. They made their own ice cream and sorbet too. Hugh liked to go down for the early sitting of dinner at six-thirty so as to not run the risk of the kitchen running out of something.

"You had a nice trip?" asked the lady driver.

"Yes, but frightfully uncomfortable. It's long and the seats get smaller and more uncomfortable every time," he answered, and felt immediately guilty for complaining about his first-class seat to this poor lady. He tried to turn the subject to her and her family, which he remembered she loved to talk about. "You had a daughter abroad. Studying medicine? She back yet?"

"Oh yes," the driver's face lit up. "She did her residency and now she is back for good. She's the oncologist at the hospital. I's real proud."

"I would be too. And will you retire now that your daughter is back?"

"Retire? Chile you don't use that kinda foul language in Carmalee's taxi. I leave you on the side of the road!" She winked at him in the mirror. "No, man. I wouldn't have a thing to do if I retired. I'd get old. When you ain't got nothin' to do round here you either end up old and dead before your time or doin' useless-fool things like gardenin' and gossip. I nuh ready for that yet at sixty-seven." He looked at the skin on her neck and the youthful glow on her face. She did not look like a woman nearing seventy. Not by a long way. "I got plenty o' time left to crochet when they take away my license."

He had to agree. Had it not been for the purpose he found in his work, he might have given up on his joints and back years ago and submitted to a wheelchair instead of the cane that got him around.

"Yuh see, nobody takes pride in they work no more." He had heard Miss Lorna repeat this mantra as well. We never had no opportunities growin' up here so when I had my own babies, I knew come hell or high water they was gon' get the best I could afford drivin' taxi. But tha's just how we are round here. My babies all gone to school and made me proud. I got one lawyer, one cancer doctor and one gettin' ready to come out of school fixin' to be a architect, all round the table every Sunday feh lunch. We's lucky people, baby. Real blessed. You only need to visit the neighbours to see how good we got it. Like the Promised Land. And old Carmalee gon' drive this here taxi till somebody take it away."

Hugh was happy to be back on solid ground, but he was remembering that Carmalee's driving did make him slightly nervous. He couldn't entirely relax as she made the wild turns of the local roads during regular and extended eye contact with him in the rear-view mirror. She also took advantage of stops at the red lights that had been installed since his last visit to look over her shoulder and make eye contact with him directly. Such a nice touch, he thought as they chatted. You wouldn't even get so much as a conversation in London. Or some other islands, for that matter.

It wasn't long before the smooth new highway deposited them at the quiet northern end of Seven Mile Beach, not far from the town of West Bay. It had once been a quiet fishing village, but now Hugh could see the tops of luxurious new condo developments and the roofs of large and grand homes that would have views that were almost as spectacular as their gardens and interiors.

The roads had improved dramatically in the decades during which he had been visiting Grand Cayman. The trip to the north end of the beach that had taken more than half an hour only took fifteen minutes now, and he had just about reached the hotel in the time it took to get reacquainted with his driver. By the time the taxi arrived at the front doors of the Corniche, the pain in Hugh's bones seemed to have all but vanished. He felt lucky to be here too. He got out of Carmalee's taxi without any help, trying to look casual as his eyes scanned for the person who was the primary reason for his trip. When he saw her walking toward him[1] , he smiled, almost involuntarily.

"You have a real nice time, dahlin," the driver said as she waved him into the lobby and got back into her taxi.

5.

When walking up and down corridors, please remember to walk along the edges (i.e. where the floor meets the walls to avoid wear and tear to runners). Please also remember to avoid walking or stepping on the edges of the Persian-type area rugs in the lobby and suites, AstroTurf or planted grass that you may encounter in the course of your day-to-day business. I recently had a most useful meeting with a former member of staff of one of the royal households who tells me that they save a lot by adhering to this simple rule in palaces across the United Kingdom!

OG

Oren Goldberg, MBE

President

The Corniche Hotel Trust Ltd.

"Keep it right ya', you hear?" Miss Lorna said to the valet as she handed him the keys to her jalopy. "I just need to pick somebody up.". She gave him a look that warned him not to comment on how out of place it would look parked among the cars of the rich and famous who were eating and sleeping at this grand resort, a few miles South of the Corniche. The double doors were opened for her, and she was given a gracious welcome. This place had money to burn. Not one but two doormen.

Lorna could not figure out if the smiles on the faces of all this manpower were in agreement with her, or if they were silently poking fun at her banger that they had been given the keys to. Or did they know that she was about to encounter something unexpected and unwelcome on this mission to collect Oren? It was hardly the first time that she had to go out of her way to collect her boss after one too many.

It wasn't even the first time that she had come to this particular resort to pick him up. It seemed like only yesterday when she had once again needed the trusted bungee cord that was kept in his glove box to truss Oren to the passenger seat. The fear of being recognized was making her uneasy. She began to feel that edgy feeling that sometimes came over her in unwelcome situations. It was a feeling that combined a sense of not belonging here, and not feeling welcome, while simultaneously being recognized and scrutinized. She could feel her skin to begin to tingle as her eyes involuntarily searched the glamorous crowd for potentially familiar eyes and gossiping lips.

Thankfully, she knew where she was going, and made her way through the lobby to the large bar. She spotted Oren as soon as she walked in. It was obvious from the way that he was slumped in his stool that he had had too much to drink to be able to drive himself home safely or legally.

"And that, ladies is how I found myself sharing a table and getting drunk with royalty, the ninth and tenth in line to the British throne." Lorna could tell from two of the four girls, seated behind him and out of his line of sight, that they were more interested in getting their bar tab paid than hearing his anecdotes of life and business in Cayman. She cleared her throat and he spun around to meet her accusing glare. "Well, ladies. It's been fun talking to you, but my dinner date has arrived. Good evening to you all." He stumbled down from his stool and led her by the elbow into the dining room.

"Oren, I came to get you and that pretentious car of yours and drive you both outta here. You didn't say nothin' about no dinner," said Lorna self-consciously.

"Nonsense. The bar tab is paid, and they are expecting us for dinner. It's the least I can do for taking you so far out of the way after such a long day."

"You mean to tell me you paid the bill for that lot?" she asked incredulously.

"Of course. They're young professional women just starting out. I see the future of this island's commerce when I advise them."

"I see the daughters of a MLA, my bank manager and two prominent lawyers. Surely you mussah known that they can pay they own bills. And they didn't come here to get business and career counsel. They was lookin' somebody to pay for a night out and some company after they get in."

The maitre d' seemed to have been expecting them, and they were led to a quiet but comfortable table. Another employee approached them.

"Good evening, Monsieur Goldberg. Lovely to have you back. We have received a delightful Chateau d... " Lorna put up her hand to stop his sales pitch.

"I will have a Chateau Red Stripe, no glass. And Monsee-ur Goldberg, a nice big bottle of sparkling water. Yuh finest vintage." Neither the sommelier or Oren argued with Lorna's instructions; the former gave a little bow and discreetly backed away.

"I thought you had a business meetin' here."

"I did. And then I stayed behind after to do some market research." He watched her as her eyes scrutinized the items on the menu, which was printed on creamy, expensive-looking paper and suspended in a linen binder. "Go ahead. You know you want to."

"To what? Take muh shoes off?"

"The filet mignon. Or take it up a notch and get the surf and turf. And for God's sake have a glass of wine. Or Champagne. If we're here on a corporate espionage mission, we need to act and behave like we belong here." The waiter reappeared, and Oren ordered a meal fit for a death row inmate, before turning to Lorna expectantly.

"The grilled capon breast and roasted vegetables for me," she said to the waiter, then turned to Oren. "I never had no Champagne before, and at these prices, I don't intend to start here."

"What do you mean you've never had Champagne before? We've got loads of it kicking around. And what on earth is a capon?"

"Nope. Never. And a capon is a castrated rooster."

"You're joking, right?"

"About what? The capon or the Champagne?"

"With all the feral chickens about this island, there should be no need to torture, mutilate and execute a poor rooster. Relax, Lorna. We're here on a mission. Think of it as training."

"This don't look like no trainin' session to me. What kinda trainin' I need now?" Lorna hated overly sentimental music, especially songs about losing one's first loves, pickup trucks, and naming songs with girls' names – all Caymanian favourites. But having to sit here in this stush restaurant was making her back sweat, and a song about dying inside had surfaced from the depths of her memory and it wouldn't go away. "I know just how the muthafucka feels."

"Pardon?"

"I say, I know just how you feel." She returned her attention to Oren and attempted a smile even though she wanted to reach over the ceviche and strangle him. She hated being forced into scenarios like this. And after all these years, Oren should have known it.

"What's the matter?" he asked in a voice of faux innocence. Oren knew all about Lorna's social anxiety. Years after first realizing what usually happened in these situations he could spot signs of it now – sometimes he suspected that he could even predict it before she felt it coming on. It usually began in surroundings she was unfamiliar with, or situations where she sensed that she had lost or was losing her social footing. He could tell tonight that he had minutes, if not moments to de-escalate the situation, even if it was happening inside his friend's head. The challenge was always to avoid any contact and conflict with outsiders where possible. Lorna had devised a clever way of dealing with anxiety while masterfully disguising it. She would invariably pretend to lose patience, or sometimes her temper, and this would allow her to leave in a huff. But Oren knew. He always knew.

"Nothin'."

"Liar."

"I don't like it when my day don't go like I planned." She felt like an impostor or intruder – Oren should have known better than to put her in this situation in such a setting.

"It's dinner, Lorna. A working dinner. Think of it as a slight change from the stale patties or conch fritters without the conch. You and I are the closest of friends and I trust you more than anyone in the world."

"Oren, you know exactly how the minds o' people on this island works. Me and you sat down her will be on the front page of the paper in the mornin'."

"Fuck 'em. No, seriously. Fuck 'em."

"Easier said. You know what'll get talked up and down the Marl Road not even a hour from now. You see that ol' whore Lorna Ebanks sittin' up in deh with her boss, puttin' on airs? You see what she was wearing? Now, who she think she is?"

"Jesus, Lorna. Surely people have more to do with their lives. We're in a business meeting."

"Business? Oren, if I was to put a match to you, you would go up in flames and burn blue."

"Okay, okay. Nuff said. You're a foodie. We both are. Let's try to enjoy this nice outing. I really didn't want to go home yet and I wanted to talk to you."

"You know I get anxious."

"Yes. Yes, I know you do. But you're fine. Everything is fine. You look very nice." Lorna had removed her apron, smoothed her hair and applied enough lipstick and dusting powder to allow her to feel comfortable. Well, comfortable enough to enter this place, retrieve and return Oren home, but not so comfortable that she could sit down and eat and drink as if she owned the place. "That was a compliment, Lorna."

"Look yah. I got sweat runnin' down my back. I can feel eyes borin' into my neck from behind, and we both know what people will think an' say when they see you an' me up in here."

"No one is watching you, Lorna. There are two cougars at the bar, and they aren't even looking in this direction. Honestly. Go ahead and look." The secret was always to find something to distract her, but never let on that he knew what she was going through, much less that he was trying to help her through it. Over the decades he had found clever ways to distract her, downplaying the external factors or lending her the social confidence to cope and stave off a full-fledged panic.

"Hmph," was her only apology as she stole a glance over her shoulder and settled herself down for dinner. He had helped her win the fight against herself, just as they had been doing for each other all these years. "Okay. Les' talk."

"Good. Now, can we stop and enjoy the Red Stripe and castrated chicken?" He waited as Lorna took a long swig from the bottle of beer.

"Whah happen, now?"

"It's bad."

"Spit it out."

"It's financial."

"It always is. But we had a good year. Or so I thought."

"Fifty per cent capacity isn't a good year."

"Well, what we gon' do?"

"I don't know."

"Last I axed, Sharon was real happy with numbers for winter. Right up to March, she said. I got that hotel school look again that she likes to use when you axe her something you ain't supposed to be smart enough to understand."

The vichyssoise was divine. It was a whipped concoction of peas, avocado, and mint blended with a few drops of truffled olive oil. It arrived in front of Lorna with a large sloppy dollop of crüme fraîche on top, and after sampling a spoonful she was tempted to order one to go as Oren's penance for bringing her here and wasting her time. She would be able to properly enjoy another helping once she was settled in front of the TV in her bare feet, and if Oren was broke (which he had been declaring for ten years), he surely wouldn't be holding business meetings in this restaurant. They had already consumed forty dollars' worth of appetizers, Red Stripe and wine.

"Speaking of Sharon, do you think I should mention the situation?

"Which one?" asked Lorna, donning what he called her *dominoes face*.

"The one arriving from Heathrow."

"Oh, that situation. Depends on how you want things to turn out. You want me to put a quiet word in her ear?"

"No, I don't think that would do. After all, we're not supposed to know. And technically you *do* report to *her*." Lorna kissed her teeth at being reminded of this. "Well it is an HR issue, isn't it?"

"Nah. Only if they shacked up under our roof. And Sharon wouldn't be that fool."

"Do you think she'll ever come out? Admit it?"

"She's a girl in love, Oren. It ain't her fault, and when you put it like that you make it sound like they doin' somethin' wrong. Only thing she done wrong was to make him stay with us, an' tha's so we don't lose no business."

"How do you know that?"

"'Cause I know Sharon. Try to leave 'em be, nuh?"

"You mean, turn a blind eye."

"Plenty rooms in plenty other hotels. You decide."

"Yeah, I guess you're right. You really should have been a mediator, Lorna. Or a family court lawyer like that lady on TV. Sometimes I wish I'd thought to send you off to hotel school instead when we had that option."

"Hmph," was Lorna's answer, which Oren knew was her way of acknowledging him without answering him in the affirmative.

"You know, you could probably still get yourself a scholarship to hotel school, or law school. I know lots of lawyers around here who are plenty dimmer than you."

"At my age? Try so hush, Oren."

"It's not so silly or crazy an idea, you know. We both know your IQ."

"We both know my age and bank balance, too."

"Fifty is the new forty. You could have a lucrative new calling ahead of you."

"How much you had to drink before I got here? I'm the housekeeper. The maid. You do this to me every damn time you had one lil bit too much wine."

"What's that?"

"Get all quixotic."

"How many maids do you know who can use that word in a sentence?"

"You know me. I like to read. And watch game shows. This is what they call a moot point in law. Nobody gon' bankroll me to go back to school now."

"Hmmm. You and me. We've put our best years, health and money into that place. We'd try walking on water to keep its doors open."

"You can say that again."

"Sorry again, Lorna. I didn't mean to delay you on the way home."

"No worries. I was waiting for the traffic to clear. Accident got it backed up all the way through Spotts to South Sound. At least you got me out before Sharon's package arrived. I been watchin' that poor fool put lipstick on top o' lipstick on top o' more lipstick all day, waitin' for Earl Grey to come."

"Have you ever stopped to think that we might have been wrong? Or at least misguided? Holding on after all these years? I mean, what do we have to show for our work?"

"Hindsight is 20/20," said Lorna, half meaning it. But she made it sound like a joke, to try and cheer Oren up, as she attacked the rooster.

6.

"Everything about the Corniche is spot-on. The food, the beach, the bubbly, and those beds are like sleeping on clouds!" –DebzOd, Cairns

Once you've worked in a hotel, a restaurant kitchen or on a cruise ship, the romance of travel, the allure of grand vacations abroad, and that love of hotel rooms or even trusting someone else to cook your dinner for you dies for ever. Your back will ache for the remainder of your professional life, the hours are longer than the legislators of the labour law ever dreamed of, and the money will never come close to paying for the hard work, humiliation and time lost with loved ones. And that's if you manage to stick to the job, rather than burning out, getting made redundant, or slipping and falling.

That was what Sharon really wanted to say to the group that she was speaking to the following morning. She was tempted. Yes, it had almost escaped out her mouth to forever scar this naive group of hospitality students. But she had just managed to repress, mainly because it would have sounded far too much like something that Lorna would say.

A young girl who had raised her hand asked: "Is there a future in the tourism industry for a young Caymanian woman willing to work and study hard?"

It doesn't really matter, does it? What I mean to say is that unless you plan to leave here and work in a destination on higher ground, you're screwed. What with climate change, melting polar ice and rising sea levels even the ski resorts won't be in business that much longer. No, seriously. Why bother? At the rate we're going? The developers on this island are hell-bent on sinking it with their plans for skyscrapers and a population nearing a hundred thousand. Then there's the coral bleaching and beach erosion and those wretched cruise ships. Our government, in their lack of foresight, are doing nothing to preserve the product that people come here to experience. Environmental protection? Who needs it? Healthcare? Nah. Education? You kids are lucky to have this class indoors, you know. But cruise ship berthing? Got to be state of the art.

"It's terrific," she answered. "The future looks bright for you, and when you find a career you love you never work a day in your life." And with that, it was time to brave the traffic and get back to her job. There was barely time to wait to be thanked, and the sounds of the young people's applause made her feel guilty, and an imposter for not even giving them the attention that they deserved.

***

So why did I choose hospitality, she said as she turned into the Corniche parking lot. A hotel is a building full of people, and I can't even pretend to care about them today.

Someone was waiting to ambush her as she came in the side door. A damage report. Mr Pratt's bed had somehow broken itself, and he was demanding an upgrade. To what? Another hotel?

There were sixty – sixty! – new emails waiting since she had cleaned out her inbox last night in anticipation of the morning school visit. She was opening the first of them when her phone rang. Whoever it was on the other end, they were lucky she was answering a call from a blocked number.

"Sharon Phelan," she snapped and immediately regretted it. For across the ether came those three words, possibly the only ones that were guaranteed to change her mood and outlook.

"Hello, my darling," sang that familiar voice.

Sharon looked cautiously around, checking no one could overhear her, then gave a hushed response. She continued trying not to smile through the brief conversation, then hung up the phone and sat up straighter in her seat.

Suddenly she felt like she could take on any obstacle that the day had in store for her.

There were days when Sharon felt downright invisible. Sometimes it was as if she simply didn't matter around here, despite being the manager of this establishment. On these days it seemed that guests and fellow employees could look right through her as if she were an apparition, stuck between this world and the afterlife. She had had a run of several days in a row when it probably wouldn't have mattered if she had come to work or not, or even if she had ended her day by walking naked into the shower of an occupied room, along with the guest. No one would have cared either way.

But today was different now. It most certainly wasn't going to be one of those days; She was wearing her most flattering deep blue two-piece, peach silk chiffon scarf about her throat; she had been told on the previous few times that she had worn this outfit that she looked as beautiful as the coral itself. She had taken an extra half-hour this morning with her hair and makeup, and it had nothing to do with the careers event. She had just been determined not to be blend in with the beige walls and travertine floors.

What amazed Sharon every day was that she had been getting away with a massive deception for so long. Every question, every invitation and every long look from one particular person made her heart flutter.

"What did you do for the long weekend?"

"We're going out for drinks after work. Join us."

"How was your vacation?"

Sharon always had her answers ready and rehearsed. Long weekends were spent at home reading. She had gone to yoga class. She had been house-sitting. She had been visiting family off-island. She had a headache. A doctor's appointment. In the past two years she had become adept at lying to her colleagues and peers. She knew that getting found out would spell not only the end of her secret affair but possibly her career as well.

She picked up her pace and was just in time to see Carmalee Goring helping Hugh out of her minivan.

"Welcome back to the Corniche, Hugh. I mean Sir Hugh," Sharon giggled as she took Hugh's offered hand and returned his smile. Hotel policy demanded that staff always greet guests when they came within fifteen to twenty feet, always with a smile and by name if it was known. Some days Sharon's face hurt from too much smiling, but today the muscles were doing it involuntarily. Her voice cracked, and she was convinced that the whole world, from Carmalee beside her to the guests down on the beach could see through her deception. It didn't help when Hugh, instead of shaking her hand, took it and kissed it before returning it to her. It would have felt slightly sleazy if done by a younger man, but Hugh had a way about him. It was an effortless sort of grace that he brought along with him when he entered a room. Suddenly the entire property felt like the hotels of her mother's primetime television shows when they would sit down and gaze into the box in the 1980s as if it was a crystal ball to another world. She checked her reflection in one of the grand mirrors without slowing down.

She had been up to the suite again to check one more time that everything was just so. She needn't have. Bobby had already unpacked the pyjamas and slippers and laid everything on the bathroom vanity in the appropriate position for a left-handed guest. The kid was impressive. One day he was going to make a better hotel manager than she would ever be. She had rechecked herself in the lobby mirror next to the suite's door, smiling at the reflection before returning to the lobby, willing herself to stop beaming. No one goes about their workday smiling like this, she had thought. You foolish woman.

She knew that Oren's parents (his mother in particular) had envisaged the Corniche as a respite from the daily business. She pointed out the special details that were committed to her memory whenever she welcomed new guests, media influencers and bloggers. There was the authentic gold leaf in the wall paint of the public areas, and the abstract sprinkling of something rumoured to be the byproduct of diamond cutting. There wasn't a sitting area that didn't boast an oriental room divider and couch slip-covered in brown canvas in the style of Coco Chanel. Every coffee table in the hotel boasted a crystal ball, brass animal or gilt box. There were three hardbound books on the coffee tables. They appeared to have been haphazardly deposited on the corner at random, but they had been carefully placed by Lorna. Sharon particularly loved the suites of the Corniche. The silk wall coverings and painted ceiling panels mimicked the blues of dusk beyond the glass patio doors.

She couldn't wait for Hugh to settle in for his latest and final stay at the Corniche. But she had yet to tell him that he would be sharing the building with the man he had once referred to as "a barnacle on the arse of humanity". Unfortunately, she hadn't been able to get out of the careers day this morning and the chances of getting out of the dinner that lay ahead were even slimmer, barring a natural disaster.

*

"Your father was at the turtle farm, bright and early this morning, front of the line and waiting for fresh meat to come from slaughter. He cooking it now. You coming here from work?"

Sharon loved all things turtle, apart from the smell of the meat cooking. Whether it was for a stew, soup or a nice steak done in garlic butter, turtle required cooking for an uncommonly long period on a very low flame and during this long process, it emitted a smell that could be less than appetizing and which was misleading about what you could expect from the final product. The preparation had been known to put off many who had not eaten turtle previously.

"What time will it be ready?" asked Sharon, hoping to miss those hours when the contents of the pot smelled like a simmering combination of mangrove water and sargassum weed. She wanted to arrive as late in the day as possible, and this would fit her schedule almost perfectly.

Hours later, her parents' house still held a trace of the lingering odour she hated so, but it was no worse than she had expected. A candle had been lit in the front room, but she knew that a cauldron of turtle stew would be sitting waiting and that she had arrived with perfect timing. Someone at the Phelan residence had been hard at work, and Sharon didn't have to ask to know that it had been her father. Growing up in this house, it had always been her father.

"Well, you's a sight for sore eyes," said her father as she kissed his forehead, careful not to disrupt his cooking. "Your mother and me had to bribe you with dinner to get a good look at yuh face or risk forgetting how you look."

"And not just any dinner," added her mother. "Endangered species."

"Well, you're looking as young as ever," said Sharon. 'In all honesty, you could be ageing in reverse. Your complexion is all youthful and pink."

"That's because he just got done chasing someone out of his breadfruit tree."

"Another one?" asked Sharon incredulously.

"The Same eediot. One no-teet West-Baya on a old orange bicycle. I fixed his ass, though. Waited at the bottom of the tree, silent as the grave and took the breadfruit off his hands before sending him on his way."

"Was the breadfruit fit to pick and eat?" Sharon and her mother both chose to ignore her father's sly reference to Bodden Town. It was his way at poking fun both at Mrs Phelan's roots in the former capital and the state of decline that meant it was all but forgotten now that the focus was on Cayman's commerce and tourism industries further west.

"You let me know. You gon' eat it direckleh."

"It's so nice to be home. And I'd gladly come here for macaroni and cheese. No need to go to any trouble."

"Maybe not ours. It would have to be the kind that your daddy makes with four kinds of cheese and truffle oil poured on the top." Sharon pulled a face in response to her mother's slight. But it was partially right. And being an adult was hard. Especially in a locale where everyone wanted to live and work, despite hyperinflation and a cost of living that rivalled the most expensive economies on earth.

"It's tough, you know. This living and working in paradise." Her parents had worked hard to provide a stable home and a good life for their daughter, despite not sharing in the great prosperity that had surrounded them this past half-century.

It had become increasingly difficult to integrate the three facets of her life, and she was apprehensive about the day when her parents might meet Hugh. Only her mother knew the truth about his life story. Even then, Sharon had saved his marriage to a wife in a vegetative state for last, hoping that her mother would find a way to spin this before retelling it all to her father and the rest of the family.

"How are things at the Lah-Dee-Dah Hotel?" asked her mother, putting on her best mid-Atlantic accent.

"Oh fine, just fine. Lots of work as always."

"And your cousin Lorna? I can't remember the last time I laid eyes on her?"

"Lorna? Oh, she's okay. The same. No change. Well, you know how she is. Even more immersed in hotel life than the rest of us. I don't know how she does it. I have to take off my hat to her. She sure does takes her job seriously. You'd think she had the most important job in the whole world."

"I guess that's one way of tackling a difficult or dead-end job," answered her mother. "I wish she would do the wise thing and use that position and proximity to rich tourists to find herself a good man."

"A good man? At the Corniche?"

"Stranger things happen in hotels, I'm sure. Lorna needs to use that position to find herself a rich but otherwise helpless middle-aged man to marry. Someone who needs a woman like her to take care of him. What do they call that? Transferable skills?"

"Mummy," answered Sharon as she shook her head and bit her bottom lip in a way that meant there was more, so much more to say. "Rich middle-aged men who stay at the Corniche are seldom looking for a woman like Lorna. And not one that looks and dresses like her – not that age and not to marry." The knowing look from her mother immediately made Sharon regret letting the conversation move in this direction. Her mother was obviously thinking about her relationship with Hugh, and Sharon knew that after a pause for effect she would be asking or making some statement the relationship she didn't approve of with a man she didn't approve of.

"So when are we going to meet this man?" her mother asked, thirty minutes after Sharon's arrival. The timing of the question only reinforced her suspicion that the family's matriarch could effortlessly read minds, even while setting a table and tossing a salad.

"Sharon, are you sure about what you're getting yourself into?" asked her mother again, after her first question was met with silence.

"*Yes, Mummy. For once I'm quite sure of what I'm getting myself into.*" This was what she would have loved to say to her mother – if only for the satisfaction it would bring her and the surprise it would bring to her mother's face...

"No, Mummy. I'm not sure. There's no playbook in a situation like this, and I don't think rules have been written for it."

"Well, in my day the rules were simple. You didn't step out with another woman's husband. Today you can buy greeting cards for the baby-daddy."

"Okay, yes. Yes. You're right. Hugh is married. There's nothing that can be done to change this fact. His wife is in a vegetative state. I would never ask him to divorce her."

"Shouldn't he be there by her side?" Sharon bristled at this question.

"He has been by her side for a decade. It wouldn't change anything. If he remained by her side it would mean we'd still be two lonely people. Don't you see?"

"You can't go nowhere with the man. You can't step out in society with him. You can't introduce him. You can't come to church with him."

"Why would I want to take Hugh to church? I mean, why would he come all this way to spend Sunday at church?"

"Worship? Fellowship?" It might offer some relief to all that pain you tell me he's in. You ever stop to consider the cause of all that pain? The source?"

"It's caused by a rare autoimmune disorder. So please don't insinuate that it has something to do with us living in sin."

Mrs Phelan opened her mouth to say something but thought better of it. There was no point.

There was no point arguing with her mother where issues like this were concerned. In her eyes, Sharon and Hugh were violating an age-old convention, so they were disregarding something sacred. And here they were on the eve of shacking up together. Her parents had never met Hugh, and unless the two couples ran into one another by chance, proper introductions could not be made without an explanation. Even if Hugh was to find himself widowed, or make the difficult decision to divorce his comatose wife, this would do nothing to change her mother's opinion of their relationship. Mrs Phelan had summed up Hugh in her mind as another married foreigner at a nice hotel in a foreign country travelling solo, looking for fun.

But after all, it was a long-standing tradition of island life, wasn't it? Middle-aged guest checks into nice hotel alone and is seen in the lobby bar five minutes later, looking for the companionship of a much younger woman (or sometimes man). The phenomenon was well documented. It was going to take some time and effort to change her mother's opinion of Hugh.

"Who wants turtle?" asked Sharon's father to a stuffy, silent room on his return.

7.

"Be sure to try the bar. We had a lovely time at the hotel. The staff were top-notch! Ask for an ocean view room. They're more expensive but worth it!"
–GFlammia

Bobby was getting sick of the case on the lounger by the beach. Stuffed into a tiny Speedo, tanned the colour of used teabags and sporting a hairpiece that he probably washed in the top drawer of the dishwasher, he was constantly snapping his fingers, talking down to everybody, chugging his vintage and demanding his glass be refilled. Still, he had "VIP" next to his name on the guest register, and Bobby would have to smile and deal with him.

Pratt had started his stay by sitting himself under the blue and white awning of the Champagne bar and trying to make friends with Bobby, finally asking in a feigned whisper "Any idea where I can score some ganja, mon?" That was a week ago, and he had come downstairs every day too late for breakfast, saddled himself up to the bar and asked for a different contraband.

"Know where I can score a bag of Charlie?"

"Who can hook me up with a bit of Molly?"

"You got any Ritalin back there?"

Bobby just pretended that they were sharing a joke, smiled, feigned a chuckle and resumed whatever it was he was doing. After a few days, Mr Pratt had finally got the hint and reverted to treating Bobby like the help. He would pick a spot as far away from the bar as possible, never stopping on his way there, then he would raise or wave his flag and order a bottle of vintage, instructing that it be kept on ice and signalling Bobby to recharge his flute on a regular basis. Today he was onto his second bottle, and clearly bored by his fellow guests who wanted to relax quietly instead of make pleasant conversation with him.

He had been on his third bottle when the girls arrived on the day before.

***

There were three of them.

They were all tall, long-legged and tanned, and as they approached the bar they turned more than just Mr Pratt's head. Bobby had seen the clique before; they were rumoured to be on the hunt for a good time, whether it be Mr Right or Mr Right Away. Mr Pratt had seemed eager to fill either of those roles; he rose from his lounger, pretending to look for a light for his cigarillo. Bobby watched the ritual with fascination. The girls ordered their drinks then proceeded to pat themselves down where pockets should have been for a means of payment.

"Put that on my tab," Mr Pratt said, as if on cue. Then began the clucking. The rest played out so predictably that Bobby marvelled at the ease with which this brown, wrinkled, lubricated old celebrity managed to become the centre of a party.

"Ladies, why don't we move this party upstairs to my suite?" he asked some time later as the sun began to set behind the horizon and the twilight mosquitoes began to awaken. Then Mr Pratt winked at Bobby, asking for more vintage and chilled glasses to be sent upstairs. It was going to be a long night.

When Pratt had departed, trailing his catch, Sharon appeared and flitted across his line of sight. "You're looking especially lovely today, Sharon," Bobby said. "I didn't know we had plans for drinks and dinner."

"And if it weren't for the compliment, I'd write you up for sexual harassment. You naughty boy. I'm far too old for you." But there was a spring in her step, and she was looking younger and more girlish today than he was accustomed to. Whatever had caused it, it suited her.

"It's going to be a long night for whoever's here. Mr Pratt has organized another party in his suite," he informed the manager. I don't know where a man that age gets the stamina."

"You have no idea."

8.

"Perfect. Everything about this place is flawless. You'll hear some say that it's dated, but if by dated they mean gracious, luxurious and comfortable, then so be it!" –JJBanks, London UK

"Sweet Jesus," Miss Lorna said, mostly to herself. Another goddammed rockstar party had obviously taken place in this suite the night before, although she knew that Mr Pratt was into some business that made him a whole lot less desirable than a rockstar. She had seen him earlier today. Stringy, unwashed hair barely concealed a bald spot at the back of his head. Expensive jeans covered a crotch that she suspected was stuffed with a sock or two, and the beaded jewellery around his neck and left wrist appeared to have been chosen totally at random. He winked at absolutely everyone he passed in the hotel, whether he knew them or not, and grinned if you were female and young.

She had been mentally and emotionally preparing herself for some years now that one day she would enter one of these suites to find one of his sort dead in the bathtub, surrounded by drug paraphernalia and wearing his last erection. She was convinced with the climbing price of accommodations that it would only be a matter of time... Fortunately, there were none of those telltale plastic bags around this morning, but there were empty bottles expensive vintage Champagne. "The things I could have done in my life with this kind of money," she said aloud. She began to pile the empty bottles at the door of the suite, counting to herself as she tried to right the madness that this man had left behind.

Miss Lorna rarely pulled out the checklist that she kept on her clipboard; she had memorized it years ago. She didn't need a list to return each room and suite to its pristine state. In half an hour the room was transformed. After moving the chairs and side tables to the east side of the suite to clean under them and ensure that there were no pills, condoms or syringes (she had found all of these and worse in her career), Lorna sanitized and polished all the handles, knobs and surfaces in sight. For quality control, she got down on her hands and knees to inspect under the sofa, or settee, as her mother used to refer to it. She stood up and opened the blinds to let in some light from the balcony through the sliding glass doors. The glass was pristine, but the conflict in the sky and sea far off on the horizon made the skin at the back of her neck crawl, which was a better augury of the weather than any barometer.

It never ceased to amaze Miss Lorna that this was the most expensive stretch of real estate on the whole island. This west-facing, windward and narrow stretch of sand would have been worthless in her grandparents' day. They would have buried their dead here or given it to poor relations because only the poor or foolish would have dared to build and live along this low-lying land along the deep unprotected Caribbean. How different life would have been if her people had held on to these once worthless coastal vistas and not the verdant inland areas where it was easier to grow cotton, mangoes and thatch for rope. If only, she thought to herself as she gazed out through the glass at the brewing sea. Maybe she could have gotten a degree, or worked in a bank, or had a condo in Florida...

"Lorna?" Sharon's voice came from the door of the suite, snapping her out of her waking dream. "Y'alright?"

On any given day she could love or hate Sharon, smile or snap at her. It depended on the situation and what she was going on about. Sharon was everything that she wasn't. They were close family and confidants, but there was a deep trench of opportunity between them. Lorna represented the old ways and Sharon the new prospects. Sharon was change and opportunity, and she didn't know it. She tried to be patient with Sharon, but the woman really could learn to speak up. "Fine, till you interrupted muh lil meditation," she answered.

"Everything okay?"

"Three condoms swimming in the toilet bowl. Mussah been one helluva night. I never woulda thought he had it in him."

"Blue pills, m' dear. Little blue pills. Suddenly old men on their deathbeds, who could only pinch our asses before, think they're young again."

"I don't need to know 'bout your life," said Miss Lorna, but immediately regretted the joke because of the look on Sharon's face: one of shock and dread. Sharon put up her hands to hide the red that was appearing on her cheeks, realizing too late what message the gesture had sent.

Lorna just sat down, and beckoned Sharon to sit with her.

"What do you know?" Sharon finally dared to ask as she willed her face to return to normal.

"I know he's a nice, decent man," Lorna began. "I know his poor wife will never wake up, and I know that the two of you make each other happy."

"And how did you come to put all this together," the manager asked the housekeeper as she smiled, finally able to acknowledge her quiet, secret happiness.

"You think I fool? I know he a good man the way he talks to me. The man is a lord or a knight or something, and he holds doors open for me. I know from the internet his wife is alive if you can call it that. And I know the way you touch up your roots before his plane lands and put on lipstick and wear your nice clothes and shoes while he's here. Never underestimate the maid. You hear? Unnah must really think I fool."

"Does anybody else know? I'd be finished. Please don't judge..." Lorna put up her hand.

"Baby, we's forgotten. We's women. Ain't nobody's business, and you not hurtin' nobody."

"We'll never be able to... "Lorna stopped her again.

"To what, chile? Marry? Shack up? You'll never have to wash his underpants or iron his shirts, so you lucky, girl. Everybody's happy and the man ain't makin' no fool of himself with a young girl the way most rich men do."

"You know Lorna, I never intended..."

"Hush chile. Nobody did, I'm sure. But at our ages we not getting' no prettier and nothing is ever quite perfect."

"Whenever we were together, it felt like the lights dimmed, crystal glasses clinked together, candles lit themselves and I could hear a simple, slow waltz being played on a piano and guitar."

"Chile, that just warmed the cockles o' my heart. That has got to be the biggest piece o' Mills and Boon bullshit I ever done heard. Even them paper packs of chemicals I put in muh lil coffee ain't that sweet." Lorna always knew that Sharon was brought up on far too many cartoons.

"You know, Lorna. One of these days, something exactly like what I just described to you is going to happen in your special, insular world. I hope for your sake the lucky person reciprocates and doesn't break your heart... Oh, one more thing."

"Yes?"

"Did you or did you not tell the new girl at the Champagne bar to piss off and present her with your middle finger?"

"Yes, Sharon. Yes I did," Lorna answered. "In fact, I told her a whole lot more and worse than that, but piss off was the only part of my tirade that fool understood. That and the sign language."

Sharon pressed her index and middle fingers into the points on both sides of her skull where her jaw met her temples. She closed her eyes and began to massage in a circular motion. "Would you care to explain to me why the young lady came to me to personally demand that you should be dismissed?"

"Yes, Sharon. Yes, I would. We was discussing our plans for the rest of the day over lunch. I said that I was planning to go north into West Bay, where I'd ordered a few pounds of turtle. Well that b... , I beg your pardon. The young lady took a turn in my ass over my consumption of turtle meat."

"So all of this stems from a difference of opinion between you and the young vegan? A cultural difference? An ideological disagreement?"

"Sharon, with all due respect, I don't understand a damn thing you just said to me. If I had gone to hotel school or community college then I would have been comfortable talking about something like culture."

"But?"

"But all I can tell you is that there's a lack of respect here. That girl just stepped off Air Canada from someplace named Shitty Creek by way o' Toronto and... "

"Stoney Creek, Lorna."

"Same shit. That chile has the audacity to call me ignorant? A savage and a monster for lining up to buy turtle meat? Legal turtle meat? Not from a poacher turtle meat? You better believe I told her 'bout her ass."

"Lorna, for the sake of peace, my sanity and both our jobs I have to ask you to do something for me."

"Yes, Sharon. I will apologize to little Miss Shitty Creek. And each o' her breast implants."

"I was just going to ask you to avoid her until she's had a bit more training in diversity and cultural sensitivity, but an apology would go a long way and it would save me the trouble of having to escalate this. And please do not address her breasts or call her Shitty Creek. Her name is Lolly."

"As in Pop?"

"Please be nice."

"I will. I can be nice. But she and I ain't done yet." Lorna forced a thin-lipped smile.

They made their way downstairs together in composed silence, both careful as usual not to say anything sensitive in a public area. They only resumed their candid conversation as they left the lobby. The other staff where eating and drinking standing up as usual while sharing gossip.

"I don't understand. Why smoke it in your room? Find a remote spot. Otherwise, you're gonna get caught or forced to share it."

"What's the gossip today?" asked Sharon.

"Somebody upstairs smokin' ganja. Middle of the day."

"Devil's weed."

"Well, then. I bet I can guess who that is."

"I take it you're not an advocate for legalizing it?"

"My body is a temple. I don't pollute it. I would never put that in my temple."

"Well I sure did," offered up Lorna, a somewhat triumphant look on her face.

"You?" they all asked in unison.

"I was a-wasting away from cancer treatment."

"So you smoked ganja?"

"I vapourized it."

"Oh, I've heard about that. You don't inhale smoke and it's better for you."

"So you don't cough so much, I guess. Are your eyes red?"

"Yeah, but to tell you the truth by the time I got my hands on a little weed, red eyes wasn't something I was worried about. The treatment feels worse than the disease. You feel like you's been put in the microwave and your cells and molecules and atoms is all vibrating and rubbing together like you' gon' combust. A puff or two slows you down and you can cope with being alive for a few more hours and another meal."

"So it really does help?"

"It don't take much. And all a sudden you got a window. A break. You feel nearly normal. You can relax. You can sleep. You can eat."

"Who'd have thought? You. Miss Lorna, the Bob Marley of our time."

"Fool. I didn't say everybody needs to be going through life smoking it every day. But when you' sick I don't see why not."

***

Visitors rarely take the time to think what an enormous difference there is between living in a large city, state or province and living on a small barren speck of land (or three specks of land in the case of the Cayman Islands), surrounded by a vast body of deep water. (The ocean around Cayman is one of the deepest bodies of water in the world). Miss Lorna could see from the expressions of the tourists in George Town that afternoon that they were all imagining what it might be like to not return to their cabins on the luxury cruise ships in Hog Sty Bay, and just stay forever. She had been asked these questions many times by many visitors to the Corniche and only after a warning from Sharon had she stopped answering with "just like bein' locked overnight inside a South Florida theme park, but with pricier food". She hated driving through town on days when ships were in port and today she was not only driving around the capital but also looking for a parking space.

"This is what hell mussah look like," she told herself. "No time an' no place to park."

She finally found a tight space, got her banking done and mailbox emptied, and then she was eager to get the hell out of town. Literally. It was on her drive home that Lorna started feeling unwell. It took her a moment to understand that what she was experiencing wasn't illness. It was jealousy. She was experiencing a pang of jealous envy of Sharon's happiness. As soon as she realized this, it soon turned to guilt.

Then she started to laugh at herself. "Fool," she said to the face in the mirror. "You got health, a head, a mouth full o' teeth, two feet and two hands. What you gon' do with another set of each?"

9.

"*****!" –Rkellehar, Florida

"Sharon? Would you do something for me?"

They were sitting up in bed, sharing the same pair of pyjamas as they had from the start. Sharon, wearing the top, looked up from leafing through architecture and interior design magazines and inserting sticky bookmarks. The drawer next to her housed a pink and yellow hi-litre marker so that she could highlight anything pertinent to the topic of outfitting and decorating the home they were planning – yellow if it was something that she wanted to return to later or pink if it was something for Hugh. Hugh, who adored pink, was sitting in the pyjama bottoms watching the news from London. Until the moment when he looked up to ask a favour of Sharon, he had barely moved and seemed not to even be breathing. He was about to ask her to scratch an area of his back between the shoulder blades that even a gymnast would be hard-pressed to reach himself.

"Stop calling you Hugh?" He looked over. Sharon was biting her lip and twirling a lock of hair, and he smiled as he took a mental snapshot of the source of his happiness on the left.

"Imp!" He broke into laughter. Then Sharon began to laugh. He always found her laughter contagious, so he laughed even harder. Then she started to snort through her nose, which made him laugh even harder and louder.

Once again, they had found themselves laughing at the memory of the night that had sparked the beginning of their love affair.

*

"Sharon darling, you can't leave me in that room," said Andrew Middleton, the handsome, stylish but very camp creative director of their Miami Agency Of Record. "I swear I'll go straight back in there and drown myself in that fucking bowl of rum punch. Whose idea was it to host this event, theme it Caymanian hospitality and flavour everything with rum? I fucking hate rum."

"Your idea, Andrew," answered Sharon. "If that wasn't bad enough, you invoiced us for the idea and called it brainstorming."

"Why do you keep disappearing for these twenty-minute pee breaks?" He looked at her suspiciously then grinned. "You've got a bag of blow up there, haven't you?"

"I have to pee. And to do that, I need to step out of this dress, then roll down not one but two girdles."

"Okay, too much information. I'm getting a mental picture. I believe you. Besides, nobody as boring as you could possibly be holding drugs. But twenty minutes? Every pee trip? How many girdles are you wearing?"

"I'll tell you when I come back down. And stop timing my bathroom breaks."

"Wash your hands. Hurry back."

"Yes, queen."

Sharon was mortified to think that she might actually be taking that much time with every trip upstairs and wondered if tonight might not be a good time to try drugs for the first time. Would they make the night go by any quicker? Could a blue pill or a red pill make the evening passable?

When they had been at school together, Andrew's nickname had been Pharmacissy, so she knew he'd have the answer. He wasn't the hardest working person in her professional circle, but he had a wit that made him fun to be around, imagination and a sharp tongue. She managed to get herself in and out of her ensemble in record time, visiting the lavatory in bare feet to give her toes a short break from the shoes that she had chosen for the evening. Then she boarded the lift for the lobby.

Before getting out the door and heading back to the event she decided there was just enough time to check her lips and blot the shine on her face. She was doing just that while balancing herself on the door when she fell forward, lost her balance and pushed the unfortunate person who was on the other side of the opening door. He bounced off her cantilevered bosom and fell head over teakettle into the arms of the couple behind him. She watched all of this happen as though it was in slow motion, but still too fast to reach out and save him.

"Oh my God. I'm so sorry. I didn't mean to mow you down."

"Good gracious, Sharon. Is that you?" She wasn't happy that the man had recognized her. She was even more upset when she realized who he was. A hasty exit stage left clearly wasn't an option.

"Sir Hugh. Dear God. I am so sorry. I could have killed you."

"I'm not that frail. Really," he said. "And you didn't so much mow me down as jump into my arms Alas, I'm too decrepit for such chivalry." He had righted, checked and dusted himself off by now, and nothing seemed to be broken. "My, how lovely you look in evening dress," he said as she helped him over to a wingback chair.

"I was just thinking the same about you in that tux," she said, noting the shawl-collared tuxedo and monogrammed patent leather slippers. She was just relieved that she hadn't cracked a bone or injured one of the Corniche's favourite guests. "You're not here for the conference, are you?"

"No, I was here on business, but I got this penguin suit out for a fundraiser. I can't remember what for and the standing has got my knees complaining." He gestured to the identical facing chair and as if on cue, a waiter asked if he could bring them a nightcap. "Would you join me for a brandy before retiring? Oh, but then you were in a hurry?"

Sharon settled herself into the chair in the corner. There was no fireplace, but they were in a cosy spot obscured from the rest of the bar by potted palms and shadows.

"Thank you, Sir Hugh. I'd love to hide out here with you here for one last drink." He smiled and ordered two large snifters of Armagnac. "Thank you, Noel." Of course, he knew his name. Did he ever forget anyone's name? "I find that a tipple of brandy right before bed helps me sleep through the pain," he said. When he smiled, Sharon admired the blue eyes and the crinkling skin that framed them.

"So, this conference," he began as he started swirling his brandy, something he did most nights as a kind of self-hypnosis before retreating to bed.

"Yes. Well, it's honestly not much more than an opportunity to court travel agents. I'm at one event or another every month trying to court luxury travel magazines, food writers and anyone else who might attract high net worth guests to the Corniche."

"You don't have a PR person then?"

"You haven't met Andrew. He's like a male version of Julie the cruise director. I mean, he's great, but PR and marketing at the Corniche is always a family affair. It has to be."

"What is it like?" he asked

"What's that?"

"Working at the Corniche. Is it more difficult than it might be because of its size than it would be at a big hotel like this one?"

"It's really quite exciting. No two days are ever the same, and I guess... I guess I get to use myself to the best of my abilities. And I doubt that it's a harder job because we're small. How can you know everybody's name and skill set in a place this size?"

"This isn't a career class. You are in no way required to inspire me to choose a career in hospitality."

Sharon laughed. "It's hard work. But it's also rewarding."

"The guidance counsellor has left the room. Now quick. Spill your guts."

"It's... well... it's... to tell you the truth, I don't know how to answer that question. You're a Corniche guest. It is unbelievably hard work. But I usually know what I'm doing."

"And it's gratifying," he added for her mischievously.

"Very." She smiled. "Everyone there is just so dedicated. The rest of the team. We're a remarkably tight little group. I think we'd have to be. To run a small hotel isn't an easy job and it's getting more difficult. But we're an uncommonly tight team."

"It shows. You're competent. Most professional."

"Thank you."

"I commend you. Your answers have been incredibly diplomatic. I'll stop being a prying busybody. And I shouldn't keep you. It's getting late."

They finished their drinks. Neither wanted to say goodnight.

"I still feel bad about what happened over there, Sir Hugh. Any faster and I'd have broken a limb or cracked your pelvis." Why was she talking about the man's pelvis? He was blushing. She knew that he suffered from a sort of painful autoimmune disease. Rheumatoid arthritis? Fibromyalgia? Someone who worked in his office or a member of his staff called periodically to go through a checklist of his needs, including linen, firm pillows, Epsom salts and slip-proof mats in his bathroom. Everyone at the Corniche knew that he loved his early-morning swims and sunshine for their effect on his limbs.

"Not to worry," he reassured her, holding his hands up with his palms facing her. His fingers were crooked, and the knuckles looked painfully inflamed. "You know, that party I was at is still going strong. I'm almost ready for bed, but I could sneak you in before going upstairs."

She declined, but something in her didn't like the prospect of him leaving her alone. "Thank you, Sir Hugh, but I'm just about done for the night too."

"Sharon," he hesitated. "Could you... I mean, would you do something for me?"

"Absolutely," she answered, hoping that it was an invitation for another chat. "Name it, Sir Hugh."

"Could you stop calling me Sir Hugh? It makes me feel like we're in a scene from Downton Bloody Abbey."

"Of course, Sir Hugh," she answered, and began to giggle as she realized the error. She tried to stop laughing, but this only made it more difficult to stop. "I'm sorry, Sir Hugh. I mean Hugh. Hugh. Hugh. Hugh." She continued to practice his name as the tears and snorting began, as they often did when she was trying to behave. It was clear that Sharon hadn't offended her companion, who by now was holding a folded handkerchief that he had fished from his lapel pocket over his mouth to stifle his laughter. Sharon held her index fingers under her lower eyelids, but it was too late. Her makeup was as ruined as her decorum. They were still laughing like this when the waiter and his manager appeared.

Sharon checked her watch. Nearly an hour had passed since her speedy exit through the elevator doors, and she was regretting that she would soon have to ride them back up to her room. This time for the night.

"Yes," said Hugh, noticing her try to hide her watch. "You must be exhausted, and here I am talking your ear off about nonsense."

"Not at all," retorted Sharon, her eyes and pupils widening noticeably. "In fact, I was going to ask if we could carry on this conversation exactly where it ends tonight."

"Would you have lunch with me?" he asked impulsively, barely believing the words that had escaped from his mouth.

What harm could it do? Surely there could be no danger in accepting his invitation for the odd lunch or nightcap in the public areas of this drab, unromantic hotel? The threat would, of course, be if someone saw them drinking together and perceived them to be having more than a professional meeting. But then again, this wasn't Cayman, and their chances of being spotted were far lower.

She nodded her head. Then they said goodnight with no fuss, both retreating to their respective rooms feeling somehow lighter, each thinking of the other.

***

"Good morning," said Sharon, not wanting to use either Hugh's name or title until she got used to calling him plain old casual Hugh.

"Good morning. Did you sleep well? For a luxury hotel, this place doesn't have beds nearly as comfortable as the Corniche."

She smiled. "I've been taking notes since I checked in as well. I always enjoy staying in other hotels to remind me of what a great product we've got. This is a five-star outfit, and there is so much that we do far better."

"Give me an example."

"We're not big enough to offer an expansive room service menu, but I wouldn't dream of sending up a pot of coffee in a glorified thermos, or without a flower in a bud vase. It's the little things."

"Yes. True. You're so adept at anticipating for your guests."

"Thank you. I'm proud of that."

They had left the high-rise hotel and made the short but slow walk around the corner to a small, dark and highly recommended French bistro. Thanks to the concierge's call ahead, they were now seated, waiting for their waiter. He and Hugh appeared to know one another's names and had a jovial chat about the weather and their health before turning to order drinks and lunch.

"An aperitif for the lady? I have a lovely rose Champagne on ice that only arrived this morning." Sharon nodded. "And a Pimm's iced tea, Sir Hugh? Or a Negroni? I will make it myself."

"Thank you, Guy. That sounds wonderful. Such a hot day." And out came that disarming smile again with the one molar larger than the other, and the crinkling of the skin around his sad blue eyes like gift wrap around a sapphire. The waiter produced a low bow and disappeared.

"I'm so happy to know that you like French food as much as I do." He said this self-effacingly, almost like a little boy with a biscuit and a glass of milk.

"I adore everything French except for the Paris Metro. Although the animal lover in me tries to stay away from foie-gras."

"I won't tell them if you don't," He smiled, and she saw once again the beautiful character and power that his face held. If he looked like this in his mid-fifties, she couldn't help but wonder what that smile might have been able to achieve thirty years ago. "And I applaud your dedication. And self-restraint."

"Don't worry. It'll pass. I'll never be a vegan, make my own granola or patchouli perfume."

"I hate patchouli. And granola. Both take me back to the washed-up hippies of my youth."

"I bet you were a fashion plate."

"Hardly. I was constantly rebelling. Everyone had too much mousse in their hair and earrings that resembled safety pins. Ah, misguided youth. What was it like growing up in Cayman?"

The drinks arrived with a small plate of amuse-bouche which the waiter placed in the centre of the table: two each of smoked salmon on tiny points of toast with dill, rice crackers piled with radish and parsley, crowned with caviar and two tiny sandwiches on their sides leaning against one another with cucumber and mint chutney.

"Compliments of Chef, Sir Hugh," said the waiter before disappearing. From his smile, Sharon guessed that Hugh knew the chef here well.

"Growing up was oppressive at times," said Sharon, accepting one of the sandwiches. "You still have to be careful who you cut off at the four-way stop or roundabout. That old person in the dilapidated car could either be your relative or a retired billionaire."

"I had always heard that it was an interesting place to live and raise a family. You know. A village and all that."

"True, true. You also had to be careful who you flirt with or you might find yourself out on a first date with your first cousin. Or worse."

"Worse than a first cousin? Or worse than a first date?

"Either. Both. I guess our parents and grandparents had good reason to fass." She had him laughing again. She liked making this sad, kind, elegant man smile and laugh. It hadn't been hard to find out more about his life via an internet search and a couple of British tabloids. He was in poor health, a lover of the ocean whose sailing had been curtailed by an autoimmune disorder. But his was a rosy prognosis compared to his wife, who had been in a coma for the past decade.

"I heard that you've had the most fascinating life," she said, trying to gently sway the conversation away from her life and in the direction of his. Salads shaped like birds' nests with little scoops of lobster in the middle arrived.

"Fascinating? Hardly."

"Certainly not unhappy."

"Bittersweet, perhaps."

"How so?"

"I'm a product of the war. I try to be grateful wherever I am and whatever situation I might find myself in. I guess your Oprah Winfrey would say I'm living in the moment."

"Were the years recovering from the war really that pivotal?"

"The decades after the war were tremendous. They were a great opportunity for some of us to learn. We had our freedom, and I suspect that was about all we had. I suppose it might have been easy to get depressed about the situation around us if anyone had known the definition of the word."

Salmon fillets arrived, grilled then chilled and surrounded by a medley of cold grilled vegetables and enormous capers, still on their stems.

"It sounds like a difficult period. And a difficult situation for learning."

"The general attitude was that we had survived and the Hun had been dealt with by the allies. There were rations, but there was opportunity."

"It sounds wonderfully British. Mustn't grumble, and all that."

"Mustn't grumble, keep calm and all that. For young people they're tea towels. But they're credos and mantras that kept us going and got us back on our feet."

"Forgive me, Sir Hugh. But you were born way, way after the war."

"Well, yes." He smiled. "Am I sounding like a relic? I don't mean to heap advice on you young people. And you've started calling me Sir Hugh again."

"Young people? You're only seventeen years older than me. Hugh."

"And how do you know that?"

"I'm usually there to meet you on arrival. I've seen your passport, Sir Hugh. I mean Hugh."

"Dessert?" Guy had reappeared, as if out of nowhere. We have a lovely crème-brulee today, made from local mangoes. Or l'assiette des fromage peut-être, Sir Hugh?"

"Je pense que non, Guy."

"Alors, du café?"

"S'il vous plait." Two cups were brought over, and coffee was expertly poured from a tall silver pot. A footed plate arrived soon after, teetering with fruit jellies, Turkish delight and tiny chocolat macarons. When the portfolio arrived at the end of their meal, Hugh was surprised to see it brought directly to Sharon without Guy so much as acknowledging his outstretched arm and hand. It already contained a credit card and chit, folded down the centre and accompanied by a black lacquered pen.

"First of all, how did you do that?" he asked. "And second, I invited you to lunch."

"I know all the tricks of the trade. And I wanted to do this. When was the last time someone took you to lunch?"

"I don't know what to say. Thank you."

"It was a pleasure. A selfish pleasure. I couldn't figure out how to invite you out somewhere again soon."

"I believe that you just did."

10.

"*****" –LDaCosta, New York

Hugh slipped on his loafers and made his way slowly downstairs for his noon meeting. He had a look of determination on his face and a sense of purpose in his slow gait.

Making his way out to the beach and lap pool, he saw his nemesis sunning himself, looking ridiculous in a tiny suit, a leathery tan and...and what the hell was that thing on his head? It looked like a badly behaved pet. Such a ridiculous little man, Hugh thought to himself. I can't believe I'm at this man's mercy.

Mr Pratt was lounging, as he usually did, next to a bucket of Champagne, spinning the contents of a flute in one hand and smoking with the other.

"Ah, Sir Hugh," he said as he saw Hugh approach, trying to sound distinguished. "Can I interest you in a glass of Veuve?"

Hugh felt as though he should have accepted, as he was paying for it. Christ, he should have brought a straw from the bar and sipped straight from the bottle!

"Thank you, no," said Hugh. "In fact, I'd like to get straight to the point, Mr Pratt."

"Very well. The point is that you have a great deal of money and I have none." Hugh had to fight the urge to reach over and strike the bastard.

"Mr Pratt," he began, "you were paid handsomely for your silence only six months ago. How can you have pissed your way through fifty thousand dollars so quickly?" As if Hugh really needed to ask. He knew how much the Corniche cost. And he was very well acquainted with the yellow label on this vintage.

"I'm afraid that silence costs, old chap." Mr Pratt replied in his terrible attempt at a British accent; he reminded Hugh of Dick Van Dyke in Mary Poppins.

"Forgive me, Mr Pratt. But this is not a business transaction. Let's call it by its name – blackmail. Which I understand is just one of your businesses."

"Oh please. Don't bore me with semantics. You have lots of money and I have none. I'm helping you by keeping your secrets secret and you're making a sound investment in paying for it."

"What a great business relationship we've embarked upon. I hope it won't always feel so... so one-sided."

Paul Pratt's smile darkened. "I'm sorry, Sir Hugh. I can't maintain a career if I'm not seen in public. And I can't go out if I'm broke. You see? Vicious circle."

Hugh wanted this conversation to be over. He also didn't want the little man to have the last word in it. "Under normal circumstances, Mr Pratt, I honestly wouldn't care. But it is rather a large amount of money you're spending. Have you ever considered either living within your means or an entirely new career path? Even if you were to switch to Prosecco and find a nice Holiday Inn... "

"I'm afraid that neither are to my taste," Pratt answered. He was enjoying this. "Think of it as a transaction, as I said. You are purchasing my silence and discretion."

"At a premium," said Hugh, reaching into his pocket for the prepared cheque. Pratt examined it, folded it and slipped it down the front of his one-sided swimming costume. Sir Hugh hoped silently that it was wet.

"I just love this place. This view. Don't you? It's easy to see what the developers mean when they say each balcony has a million dollar view."

"True. It almost makes one want to work harder. Or does it?"

"Ah. Yes. Work. You know I was once rather successful."

"Yes, I've seen that show where they lock you up in the house with the hidden cameras. I understand that you used to be some sort of celebrity or entertainer. Too bad it doesn't pay better," Hugh prepared to end their meeting, hoping to leave with a blow where it hurt most.

"Reality television and commercials don't pay, unfortunately. Neither does the stage. And my matinee idol days are recently behind me. But I'm hopeful..."

"So am I, Mr Pratt. So am I. I'm hopeful that we never hear from you again. This relationship is costing me more than the one that I actually enjoy."

"A mere fifty grand, Sir Hugh. I doubt you'll even miss it. You and your lady friend do tend to stay in most evenings together, I've noticed."

"Make it last," said Hugh. They didn't shake hands. The meeting on the beach had lasted far too long for Hugh's taste and he regretted the fact that it had taken place in public. He didn't want anyone thinking that he and Pratt were friendly, much less that they knew each other socially. He would have preferred not to know the pathetic little man at all. He found Pratt entirely distasteful. He dressed like a teenager, spent Hugh's money like royalty and there were several unpleasant stories of his drunken spectacles, orgies and mishaps involving an audience, often in the Corniche's lobby.

Hugh couldn't help but wish that the wind, which had been picking up all day, would blow that ridiculous thing off the top of Pratt's head and out to sea.

After he had left, Pratt also retreated upstairs, to run a bath and have a long celebratory soak with a glass of Champagne. And maybe a line or two to wash it down while he got ready for the evening's festivities...

11.

"Flawless!" – GiuseppeF, Naples

Another day, another dirty hotel. Lorna had arrived before the sun as she always did, menthol cigarette in mouth and ready to take on whatever mess lay ahead. She left one room and knocked at the door to another, entering cautiously. A lovely smell of roses wafted towards her as she did a quick scan to make sure that she wasn't interrupting old Mrs Smythe's beauty routine or television time, or one of the couple's naps.

Years of looking after the Smythes had painted a clear picture for Lorna of a happy couple's life together. Well, at least their evenings. They came to Cayman every winter for a week or two. They rarely stayed in for dinner but always returned early. Mr Smythe would have a brandy before bed while he watched the news and Mrs Smythe would use the better part of a pot of rose-scented cold cream and a bag of cotton balls to remove what little makeup she wore and clean her face for the night. Sometimes Mr Smythe would fall asleep in the chair, brandy in hand. All these little rituals were easy to piece together, although Lorna was never around to witness them. It must be so unbelievably liberating to have that much time on your hands, that you could literally clean your face with cotton balls and cold cream.

Every year Mrs Smythe would seek her out and greet her like an old friend, saying "Lorna, it's so nice to see you again." Nice people. Old school. They were the kind of people who would never leave a mess behind, tidied up their own beds and hung up their towels. They also left behind a bottle of expensive perfume or an envelope of cash for her, in addition to the generous gratuity that went into the pool. They'd been coming for as long as she could remember and Lorna always made sure there was a large bowl of cotton balls on the vanity and good brandy in the bar, waiting for their arrival.

This room had been a breeze. She had needed less than ten minutes in it before backing out, leaving one last spritz of lavender floating in the air before closing the door. And now from her favourite guests' room to her least favourite. What lay ahead now was whatever mess Mr Pratt had left behind for her before he went downstairs to sun his leathery body. But her phone rang as she was letting herself out of the Smythe's suite. It was Sharon and she was hysterical.

"I just went home to walk the dog and my electricity is off."

"Did you pay the bill?" asked Lorna, wondering if she wasn't asking the obvious. She knew better than to bother asking about the fuse box.

"Well, not exactly," was Sharon's answer. Typical. "The bill was ginormous. And I was waiting to get paid." Lorna wasn't surprised. Everybody's monthly utility bill was high in Cayman, but Sharon owned every appliance known to man and had something plugged into every socket in her little apartment. There was that machine in the kitchen to roast, grind and brew the beans for a single cup of coffee, then there was the basket of every kind of hair what-it-name in the bathroom: one to blow dry, another to straighten and yet another to render hair corrugated like an old-time zinc rooftop.

"Well, if you didn't pay the bill you need to go line up now at the accounts desk, or you'll end up at that gas station tonight in Industrial Park and... "

"Oh that's Hugh on the other line," said Sharon, cutting her off mid-sentence. "I'll call you back." And she was gone. Just like that.

"Good luck doin' your hair and makeup for dinner in the dark," said Lorna to dead air and put her phone away. She knew how hard it was to get by in Cayman, but she still found it difficult to sympathize with Sharon, who made triple Lorna's salary. Other than fertilizer and orchid food, Lorna made few extravagant purchases and she sure as hell wasn't going to get up and spend two hundred dollars like Sharon did every other Saturday morning to have some white man straighten her hair, hide the roots and convince her it needed to be longer, darker or conditioned like they did it in Brazil.

It wasn't that Lorna didn't care for Sharon. They were cousins and no matter how different they were or how much Sharon annoyed her she would always love and worry about the girl. But she was a grown-ass woman and able to make decisions for herself. She had managed to go away on her own to that fancy hospitality school and come home with the degree and speaking French. This was no small achievement for a Caymanian woman whose parents had never seen the inside of a lecture hall or dared to dream of a real career. But sometimes Lorna could swear that them people had sent Sharon home book-smart and life-stupid. She would forego putting even a few dollars away for shopping weekends in Miami. She had every cosmetic known to man stacked away in her bathroom, and dinner reservations for every Saturday night for the next month. Just last month, Sharon had declared to Lorna that she was going to a new church, not a surprise as she seemed to belong to the church of the month club. But her reasons had annoyed Lorna.

"You mean to tell me that you gon' up and leave the Church o' God that you and I was brought up in for some jump-up church in Prospect because they got better dressed white people in they pews?" she had asked accusingly.

"It's not that, Lorna. I said that people dress better at this church. It's not the same thing. I like their sense of community. And at least I get dressed up to show my face before God on a Sunday morning. You should try it. People talk." Sharon probably hadn't intended this to come out the way it had, but it had stung Lorna nonetheless. It had felt like a light slap to the face. Lorna had said nothing more.

She wasn't ashamed of her Sunday morning ritual. She sat in her garden with her orchids and read about Buddha and meditation (she couldn't see the point in actually sitting there with her eyes closed doing nothing) and other people's holidays, like Diwali. She didn't know if there was a God, if he was a man, or if he was white, but it seemed like a waste of his precious time for people to be going to church to ask for things like money or a Mercedes Benz or a man to come rescue them. If she wanted a German car she could drive herself into town and ask to see her bank manager for a loan. The chances seemed a whole lot better that way.

Lorna had hoped that the company of a mature man like Sir Hugh might have grown Sharon up a toops. She was half-surprised that she'd managed to hold on to him, much less keep the relationship on the down-low. This new church wouldn't last long though. Sharon was bound to convert to Anglican next month in case Hugh's wife were to die and she had a half a chance to become the next countess or baroness or whatever would happen if she was to marry Sir Hugh. Then she'd be Lady Sharon and have the whole family curtsying to her But that was Sharon, and Lorna wasn't about to change her any more than Sharon was going to get Lorna to wear a dress on a Sunday morning to impress a pile of uppity white Baptists.

"Mr Pratt? It's Lorna. Lorna from housekeepin'," she sang as she knocked lightly on his door. She knocked again before letting herself in with the plastic pass key that she kept tethered to her uniform. At least there were no additional guests in the bed today, and she hadn't crashed a party. Lorna was used to taking pandemonium and turning it into the calm beauty that one expects from a room at a boutique hotel, but this was too much.

"Suh hep muh Crise."

The room was a battlefield, objects flung everywhere. Sitting among the carnage was the infamous guest himself, facing a laptop that was playing an orgy scene. Red-faced, sweating, twitching and wearing his bathrobe over his clothes, Mr Pratt looked as though he hadn't left the room in days. And he didn't seem to have noticed her despite her repeated theatrical throat clearing. She went straight into her monologue.

"I'm terribly sorry to have disturbed you, sir." She said, sounding like something off the TV. Pratt didn't hear. She should probably take the opportunity to back out of the mess, close the door silently behind her and hope that nothing would snap him out of the deep thoughts that were preoccupying him before she escaped. But the man was in a pathetic state – she didn't need a closer look or a degree to know that. He seemed to be talking to himself, but nothing audible was escaping his lips. There were white peaks of dried saliva at the corners of his mouth, and his lips were as red and dry as the rest of his face. Long lines of white powder sat on the coffee table with a razor blade, a credit card and a big bag of the powder.

There was something seriously wrong here. She should have called someone else, maybe even an ambulance. But now Lorna saw that there were plates and mirrors piled with white powder and little white bags of more everywhere. It wouldn't end well for either Pratt or the hotel's reputation if she were to call for help.

"Mr Pratt?" There was no answer. "Okay, baby," she said as she lowered herself into the seat next to Pratt. "Miss Lorna here to help. We gon' get you fix-up."

Something, whether the weight of her sitting down next to him or her hand on his shoulder, jogged him out of his daze. He jumped, which made her squeal with surprise. He pushed her back and climbed on top of her. Both his body and breath had the odour of someone who hadn't seen soap or water in days. His breath was so pungent that it was bordering on sweet. She could smell his armpits and they reminded her why she hated cats.

"Yeah?" he half asked, half ordered as he gnashed his teeth and pointed unfocused eyes towards her. Before she knew it his hands had circled her wrists and her fists had been restrained near her ears. "Yeah? You like that, bitch?"

Madman or not, drunk or high, nobody called Miss Lorna of the Corniche a bitch. She locked eyes with him. All her concern and patience were both gone, at one and the same time.

"Look yah. You need to get off me. You hear? Or I gon' fuck you up." Her stern warning didn't have nearly the effect she had been hoping for – she could feel the adrenaline building and sweat accumulating on her limbs.

"Yeah? You like that? Don't you, bitch?" Again with this fuckery. Why did men assume after a few minutes of internet porn that they had the right to mount and penetrate the nearest woman?

"Like this? Like you?! You's a fuckin eediot…" she was about to add madman to this but realized that he had her overpowered. He began to flatten the palm of his hand over her mouth. Now she regretted not screaming in the first place. Most people underestimated the strength of Lorna's slight and wiry frame. She had never looked in the direction of Pratt and assessed him for potential harm, yet here she was, lying underneath him, unable to move, unable to scream. She made a mental note to insist on a panic button as soon as she was out of this predicament.

"We're gonna have a real good time, you and me," continued Pratt. His free hand was beginning to search down her body seeking buttons and zippers. In reply, she brought her knee to his groin and smiled grimly at the sensation of the wind departing his lungs. Then she bit the fingers that he had been attempting to stuff into her mouth, hoping that she would have enough time to scream when he removed his hand. Resisting him had tired her out more than she had realized. She was sweating and panting through her nostrils and couldn't catch her breath. Fucking menthols.

Pratt let out a yelp and removed his hand to examine the fingers she had bitten. Lorna tried to scream but nothing would escape her parched mouth and throat. Then an impact from the back of his hand left an imprint of stars behind her closed eyes.

"You fucking bitch," he growled as his pelvis once more began to grind against her. His hand began to tug against buttons and zippers.

"Dear God," she whispered. It was a name she didn't call often: there was so rarely an answer. But his hand was now at her collarbone, squeezing, and she suspected that she might not be conscious for much longer. "Oh Jesus."

She turned her head away. On the coffee table next to the laptop sat one of the solid glass crystal ball paperweights that were everywhere around the Corniche. It was hard and heavy enough to incapacitate him with a swift blow to the head, maybe even knock him out. And as if in answer to her prayer, some source outside her own mind seemed to draw a red dotted line with an arrow at the end between the ball and Pratt's head, with the trajectory, speed and an x on the exact spot where she might make contact.

The first impact with the side of his face was satisfying, knowing that she had knocked some of that expensive dental work out of his mouth. He recoiled but she pounced, making up the distance.

"Motherfucker!" The second blow was twice as satisfying. His nose would never look as pretty again. But it was the third blow meeting his skull just above the ear that brought the most satisfaction, along with a cracking sound that made her think of the need to stop at the supermarket for eggs on the way home. He dropped on the floor like a puppet whose strings had been cut.

"That," she said as she stood over him sweating and panting, pulling down her apron and smoothing her hair. "That was for my sister maids everywhere. You think yuh man now?" She pushed her toe into his side to get his attention. There was a lack of tension in his body that she hadn't been expecting. "You shoulda known better," she warned the unmoving pile at her feet. "And I done told you not to fass with me, you hear? It ain't like I didn't warn you."

Pratt was out cold. She decided to turn him over so that he would see her face as soon as he came to and she could really tell him about his ass. She found that the spot above his ear had gone slightly concave and the area around the corresponding eye had swollen with alarming speed. Something was oozing out of his mouth and nose that was going to be a pain to clean up. She considered calling an ambulance, but it could take a good half an hour for one to get to the Corniche this time of day. And she knew from the mess at her feet on the floor that she need not bother with the call. The motherfucker was dead. If he wasn't, he would be pronounced dead by the time he reached the George Town Hospital.

"Sh-sh-sharon?" she managed to stammer into her phone once her hands had stopped shaking enough to allow her to dial. "Goddammit, Sharon. You nuh gon' believe this."

"I'm still on the other line with Hugh. Can I c—" Sharon was cut short by the sound of the sob that came from Lorna's mouth. Lorna was surprised by the involuntary sound herself.

"Sharon, I need you to get off the phone and come up here now. You hear me? Please." This plea them both. It was the first time in recent memory that either of them could remember Lorna admitting that she might possibly need another person's counsel, comfort or help. She put down the phone without cancelling the call and lowered herself onto the Chesterfield, trying to regain control of her body and stop the shaking that had overtaken her.

12.

"Thanks for everything. Can't wait to come back." –CParsons, UK

"I've dealt with him, darling. There's no need to concern yourself," said Hugh into the phone next to the bed.

"For now. He'll tear through that fifty thou in no time at all, what with the way he likes to live," Sharon answered, not entirely convinced that they had weathered the worst of Hurricane Paul's destruction.

"It was worth it. It will buy us some time. You're not to worry, Sharon. I've taken care of Pratt."

"I'm so sorry, Hugh. It's so much money. I don't even know how to wrap my head around such a number. What will we do? Keep paying him off?"

"I've asked you not to worry." But Sharon worried. Mr Pratt had expertly made himself the single greatest obstacle to their immediate happiness. She cursed the day that he had first arrived at the double doors of the Corniche; it was hard to believe that such a turd of a man could make such a huge pain of himself.

"Now you can start worrying about china patterns. And thread counts. And paint chips and water glasses," said Hugh.

"Oh, that's Lorna on the other line. Of all the times to block my *qui*, she had to pick now. I'll call you back in a minute, Hugh." But following the urgent summons from Lorna, she realized that this wasn't the moment for that.

As was on the way to Pratt's room she wondered what the hell it was gonna be today? Contraband? Another orgy? She made her way from the cramped back office to the front of house and reception desk. As if on cue, a sour, surly and unsmiling face approached and popped a card on the marble top of the raised desk, apparently to check in.

Millicent Myles," announced the owner of the face. Sharon smiled and nodded in preparation for welcoming the woman to the Corniche but instead she presented her identification and credentials, then continued. "I'm from the Board of Tourism. Random room inspection. Tag you're it and lucky me."

"Of course you are," Sharon said through her grin as she looked down – it wasn't a credit card, but the woman's photo ID and credentials from the regulatory branch of the statutory authority of the Islands' Government. "Would you excuse me, just a moment? We'll have a showroom ready for you, directly. If you would care to wait in the lobby...? Can I get you a..."

"Per policy, I'm not allowed to accept refreshment. I've also come with a list of rooms generated at random. Unless they are occupied, you are required by law to show them to me. We're checking drains. Legionnaires' Disease, you know." Sharon's mobile phone vibrated in her pocket again. It was Lorna. Again.

13.

"Tropical Storm Lisa Looks to Disrupt Cayman Islands Winter Season"

"Have you ever wondered why they put potted plants in pretty pots absolutely everywhere when they're decorating these places?"

"No, not really."

"I have this theory. Once upon a time, there was this decorator of hotels whose aesthetic was bush jackets and pith helmets. This decorator went from grand hotel to grand hotel to do their interiors in the most exotic style of the day. That style stuck as the gold standard for hotel interiors and today concierge floors everywhere emulate the Bengal Bar at the Empress Hotel."

"Oh?"

"Then they got to the end of the project and realized that the corners were too bare. They had already blown the budget on stuffed tigers, mahogany wainscoting and authentic African tribal spears and shields and shit. So they had no choice but to put palms in brass and blue celadon pots and place them everywhere. Like some sort of indoor landscaping."

Oren sat picking at a rather anaemic looking garden salad and hoped that Louis Bodden was close to getting to his point. If he had one. He had been going on about the evolution of hotels for the best part of an hour now, and clearly considered himself a connoisseur on the topic. As if staying in a lot of hotels had made him some sort of hotel expert. He had an idea of what Louis was getting at but was feigning stupidity in the hopes of getting through lunch without hearing the pitch again.

Louis found the Corniche dated, past its prime. He was trying to tell Oren in this roundabout way that change was inevitable. The lovely lunch was a subtle bribe to somehow get Louis involved in returning Oren's beautiful old hotel to modern prosperity.

"It's closed now, you know."

"The Empress?!" Oren had no idea. Times must be tough.

"No, Oren," answered Louis, slightly exasperated that Oren hadn't been following his line of logic. "The Bengal Bar. But mind you, the Empress has changed hands a couple of times too these past few years. A lot has changed since the days of the old Canadian Pacific."

"So maybe we could get all those old zebra skins and stuffed cats and tribal weapons and stuff on the cheap."

"Now why would you want to do something like that?"

"You know. Make the Corniche a little more tribal. An African theme."

"I'm going to tell you why that's a bad idea," said Louis, leaning forward. "If that theme put a hundred-year-old institution out of business because the management was unwilling to change with the times and stay on top of hotel trends, why the hell would we want to follow suit?" Oren didn't when Louis had joined the Corniche's management, but suddenly he was using *us* and *we* whenever he talked about it. A subtle manipulation tactic. The bastard.

"I guess you're right," answered Oren, thankful to see another course being placed in front of them. "I have the distinct impression that there is absolutely no conch in these conch fritters. Just flour, cornmeal and shallots fried in a ball. More like a cornmeal dumpling."

"I think they're quite lovely. They're light. Light and very flavorful," observed Louis.

Oren couldn't help but think to himself that only Louis Bodden could enjoy something so lacking in substance as these theme park conch fritters. They reminded Oren of that one time that Chef had made something from a recipe he had found online called mock turtle soup, made with ground chicken breasts. "So why the hell don't we just call it chicken breast soup?" Oren had asked. "If you want to do a turtle soup, call the turtle farm and place an order." Was this what hospitality had become? The same print in every room across the world and bedspreads that were only laundered every eight weeks and carpets that you're afraid to allow your bare feet to touch? Maybe Louis had a point. Perhaps it had all become more about the real estate, the spa and artisanal cocktails.

"You might have a point about the hotel. Maybe it's time to make some changes."

"Of course I'm right. I know what I'm talking about."

"Remind me again, Louis. How many times have you done this before?"

"What?" asked Louis, wide-eyed.

"How many times have you spearheaded a hotel project like this before? Transformed one. Or brokered the sale and purchase of a hotel site? Or overseen the redevelopment of a place this big?"

"I'm not a hotel developer, Oren. As you know, I'm a real estate guy. I'm a dealmaker. I don't traditionally do hotels. But you're my friend. We're friends and I want to help. Especially before it turns out to be too late."

Sure you do, Oren wanted to scream. You're already in hot water over unregulated funds, a court case over the ownership of dozens of acres of land in East End, a marina project that had gone belly-up and a memo of understanding that was full of holes involving as the frontman for a South-Asian developer of airports that you tried to sell to the local government...Sure, you want to help me. I only need to sign on the dotted line.

"Thanks, Louis. I'm so grateful for your guidance." No reason to rock the boat and have to pay for his own lunch as well. If he continued to lubricate Louis' ego, there might well be a bottle of buttery Chardonnay in Oren's near future. Yeah. Why rock the boat now, before the mains had even arrived?

The half of Oren's heart that actually minded Louis practising his reptilian pitches knew that things could not be allowed to continue as they were. He would be a fool not to accept that money was scarce and getting scarcer in this new economy. He would be a total idiot to not admit that something had to give. And soon. But he'd be even stupider to sign anything that Louis Bodden thrust at him as a solution to his problems, whether it was a bill of sale, a consulting agreement or anything in between.

"I'm a dealmaker, Oren," reiterated Louis. "And what you have here is a deal dying to be made." Honestly. How did he come up with this dealmaking bullshit? Those slippery one-liners that he recited without so much as a hint of irony in his voice and that weasel-like, lopsided smile on his face. Behind Louis a giant, ugly iguana was slowly approaching, probably to find out what they were eating, and whether they might be in a sharing mood. It stood on the low stone wall under the thatch tree, unmoving and unblinking. Oren couldn't help but find this face more welcoming, more friendly and more believable than the face of his lunch companion .

"Now, then," he continued. Back to this hotel project of yours?" Oren knew what Louis was attempting to do here. He was trying to broach the topic of the Corniche from another direction. His pan-fried wahoo arrived in time to allow for a change in topic.

"It's a lovely place, Oren. Nobody is contesting that. But you're running on an antiquated business model." Louis Bodden seemed to get into the same argument with Oren whenever they met. Oren would lament at the cost of doing business on an island, the competitive nature of the industry, or the high cost of labour or food. Louis would suggest what he always did: tear down the current building and put a ten-story mid-century modern structure on the land, then reap the profits.

"You're asking me to do the unthinkable, Louis." And it was unthinkable to Oren. Louis was taking advantage of lunch today to raise his case again, specifically the case for redeveloping the Corniche site to allow it to accommodate far more drinking, dining and stayover guests. He had crunched numbers for Oren more than once.

"The hotel currently has, what? A few dozen rooms and a handful of suites?" Oren nodded, not wanting to bother to correct Louis with exact numbers. Louis went on to lament the size of the Corniche's 35-seat restaurant that needed to offer two dinner services in order to break even and serve guests' demands, a charming but tiny Champagne bar, and a lap pool that Oren admitted had been an afterthought.

"Or add five stories. That will double the room count, if you must. But I wish you'd consider the merits of a demolition and rebuild."

"But it just wouldn't be the same, Louis. Our guests wouldn't come back to a Corniche that's twice the size." Oren knew his demographic well. They didn't want to be elbow-to-kneecap in matchbox rooms They came for comfort and privacy and more than a touch of opulence. "But you're right. We have not changed a whole lot." Almost everything remained in the original style in which it had been designed and built, which the long-dead architect had coined British-West-Indian-cum-Hollywood-regency.

"And you know what? A redeveloped Corniche site would attract a different category of guest altogether. New guests. Young guests. Come on, Oren. You're saying no to a young, rich niche of consumer?"

"I can't conceive of it, Louis. I just can't. Maybe after I'm dead and gone." This was a comforting thought to Oren. They could do as they pleased once he was gone, these young people with their spas and parking garages and Instagram. "Is it me, or do we have this same conversation every time we meet up?"

Over the years they had met for lunch, drinks or cards once or twice every month. Louis preferred one-on-one chats to the regular card parties. He did not trust that facety maid; she was against the redevelopment of the Corniche. She sang the same asinine love song to the hotel as her boss. She was also far too good at cards. And dominoes. They were a tight little set, the staff of the Corniche were...

Today Louis persisted.

"I could put a deal together in a morning, over lunch and a few phone calls. With a piece of beach that beautiful, that valuable, I could probably raise the seed money over lunch alone..."

Oren put his hand up to pause their conversation as he answered his mobile phone. It was Lorna, saving the day and giving him a thankful excuse to end their lunch meeting and this discomforting conversation.

"Ummm, sorry. I'm going to have to cut this lovely lunch short. As usual, something's gone wrong back at the hotel."

14.

To: All
From: Oren Goldberg
Re: Local Geography

When welcoming guests, giving directions or making recommendations, please remember to refer to places (especially our island) by the correct names as it drives me crazy hearing places not referred to or pronounced correctly. This includes envelopes. For instance, it's George Town and not Georgetown (Guyana is some miles away), Grand Cayman (rhymes with gay-man and not hey-mum) and the Cayman Islands or just Cayman. Not the Caymans and certainly not the Grand Cayman Islands as I keep hearing and recently spied on another hotel's lobby mural.

Let's all play our part at consistency, shall we?

OG
Oren Goldberg, MBE
President
The Corniche Hotel Trust Ltd.

Sharon knocked on the door of Mr Pratt's room. Lorna opened it, careful not to be seen from the hall, then retreated to a corner and slid down the wall to a seated position.

"Oh God. What now?" Sharon asked. What maintenance issues or crisis had brought her upstairs? She was confused by Lorna's body language and studied her as she waited for an answer. "Are you alright?"

"No." Lorna's voice cracked and she was unable to get another sentence out.

"What's the matter?"

"Look there," was the short answer. She was crying quietly, but trying hard to hide it. "Over there," she said again emphatically, pointing with her chin. Sharon walked over to the mess of dirty linens and lifted a corner. She stifled a shriek and backed away instinctively.

"Oh my God. What the fuck... I mean, who the fuck?"

"Who you think? Pratt."

"Is he okay?"

"No, Sharon. He is not okay. The man is dead. Wha' the hell do you think?"

"Why didn't you call the police? Or an ambulance. When you found him like that.. "

"He don't need no ambulance, tha's for sure. And I didn't find him like that. And if I was to call the police, they gon' arrest me."

Lorna looked as if she had been in a schoolyard fight and lost. Her hair was dishevelled, her face red, and her eyes bloodshot. Had she fallen on her face?

"You mean... you mean to tell me that you did this?" Her voice rose to a falsetto as she began to add up the variables and guess at what had happened in the room before she came in. Now it made a little more sense. She had entered a crime scene. Lorna and Pratt had been in some kind of physical fight, and Lorna hadn't lost.

"Are you sure he's dead?"

"Dead as an iguana in the middle o' the road."

"How can you be so... "

"Sharon, nobody can not be dead with no pulse, and they brain comin' outta they nose."

"Lorna, what have you done?" Her hand instinctively came up to cover her mouth and she backed away from Lorna, before realizing that this took her closer to the body and taking a few panicky steps in the opposite direction.

"Don' worry, boss. I's all don' killin' for today." Lorna looked up at Sharon and attempted to reassure her with a tiny smile. Sharon had never seen her in a state like this, all unkempt, pathetic and confused.

"I should call somebody. I guess I should call Oren," she said to nobody in particular. For once Lorna had followed the chain of command by calling her first, but Sharon wished that she hadn't this one time. Instead of calling anyone she slid down the wall and sat next to Lorna who had taken out her own phone and began to dial, clearing her throat.

"Sorry to bother you but could you come back here? It's real urgent. Yeah, baby. Somebody here you need to see. Okay. We gon' be here waitin'. No, nothing I could explain over the phone. Even if I tried. Even if I wanted to." She put the phone away and began to speak to Sharon.

"He came at me first. Honest. True to Crise. I thought the worst he was gon' do was rape me when he grabbed me, but when put his hands around my throat I thought he was gon' kill me. If it wasn't for one o' them damned obeah balls he'd a' done both. So no. No. I ain't alright."

"Of course he came at you first. I'm sorry. It was just the shock of seeing a dead body there like that. Really, Lorna. I'm sorry. Of course he did. You were defending yourself. Maybe we still need an ambulance for you. Do you need to see a doctor?" She awkwardly put her arm about Lorna's shoulders as Lorna crouched her head deeper between her knees and began to heave, shake and rock herself. Sharon pulled her closer, thinking that this was probably the first time that she had ever been required to comfort her cousin.

"No. I only need a Valium. And if you look around this room he got plenty o' that."

Lorna continued to cry quietly while trying to retain any dignity she could muster. Sharon had never seen her cry, even in times of mourning. They stayed this way for several minutes before Lorna sat up, attempted to smooth her uniform and her hair, then winced as she tried to get up.

"Where are you going?" Sharon immediately regretted asking yet another question. She knew she sounded as if she was gathering information for an inquest. She guessed it probably made her look uncaring, as if she suspected that today had been the day that Lorna finally snapped at being asked for extra towels or shampoo, mangling the first unfortunate guest that she had come across.

"Balcony. I need a cigarette." Sharon helped her to stand up and took her by the shoulders, guiding her out the glass doors and onto one of the reclining sun loungers, then sat down next to her and waited for the cigarette to be lit before taking Lorna's free hand. They sat like this for the half-hour that it took Oren to arrive, only moving when Lorna needed her hand back to light another cigarette or wipe her eyes. She lit four more cigarettes as she sat crying, always returning her hand to Sharon's as they waited.

"I wus thinkin' about quittin' smokin' on my way into work this mornin'. Real glad I didn't pick today to do it. True to Crise." She stared out. Seven Mile Beach was beginning to dim its lights for the sunset show; the crisp blue of the sky and ocean was deepening around the edges to purple as the sun started to sink into the Caribbean. It was like looking into the mouth of a conch shell.

"You know the way the sun sets right here is truly something that demands you stop and look. I don't know why I don't think to look up and enjoy it more often. Even in this foul weather the sky is beautiful." Sharon was trying to keep the conversation light until Oren arrived, but Lorna didn't respond and they descended into an awkward silence.

There was a light knock on the outer door. Sharon popped up, and Lorna was relieved to see that she was lucid enough to check the peephole before opening the door. She could hear Oren's exasperated voice as he came in. "I swear to God, if we find any more mold in this place I'm gonna take a match to it and retire on the insurance payout. If it's not one thing, it's your mother. What did you say – holy shit." Lorna looked over to see Oren steady himself against the wall as the colour drained out of his face. Sharon was holding up a corner of the sheet, as if in an episode of Quincy. "Is he... you know... is he...?".

"I sure as hell hope so," said the housekeeper as walked back into the room and sat wearily back down on the floor, then patted the floor next to her. The Corniche's owner slid his back down the wall and sat down, as Lorna had a few minutes earlier. "And we thought the weather would be our biggest problem this week." She began to cry again.

"Weather? What weather?" Oren began to laugh, his laughter taking on a hysterical tenor – tears began to run down his face. Sharon could see that despite his shock at seeing a dead body, Oren's presence had done a lot to restore Lorna. They sat hugging one another, one in shock, the other in hysterics.

"Oren, I know how you must feel. It's been one bitch of a week. But it can't be as bad as all that," Lorna said as she squeezed the hotel's patriarch. But she suspected that it was that bad, and the dead guest was the last straw. The cherry on top of a fast-melting dessert.

Oren made no effort to hide his emotions, but that seemed to galvanize Lorna's self-control. "You want a menthol?" Sharon watched as he accepted one of the cigarettes out of the pack, took one of the long feminine cigarettes and accepted a light. She had never seen him smoke.

The sight seemed to cheer Lorna up too: "It always makes me laugh when I see you smoking my menthol slut-sticks. Now tell me. Wha-gwan? You kill somebody today too?" He shook his head: the gesture didn't seem intended to answer her question, but to bring some clarity to his thoughts. "This ain't the first dead body you and I have had to tend to. Wha' the matter with you? What makes this any worse? You think anybody'll miss this damn fool?"

"No but this one is murder, not natural causes. The news would be enough to finish us off, once and for all."

"Come on now, man. It's about to kick into high season. It's been slow, but we had slower Octobers than this. It can't all be as bad as this," Lorna said, her eyes wide as tried to convince him – and herself – that everything would be fine.

"It's worse, Lorna. Truly. Bad. It's not so much the body, although I honestly didn't need something like this today. But it is enough to finish us off. Easily."

"Now you and I know the man was up to no good. He was a bad man. Did you notice the desk over there? It's piled high with cash, pills, bags of white powder. I don't think we're gon' find any vitamins or washin' powder over there. Do you? All we ever did was put him up. He paid his bills and the only thing to miss about him is the bar tabs."

"Up to no good. You can say that again. He and Ms Davis had been using us as a corporate office for years. But you're right. They drank a lot of Champagne. I always knew that there was more to his visits and their presence. But we needed the money. And he did bring a certain D-List celebrity along with him. Such a childish obsession with being called by name, room upgrades and yellow labels."

"You can say that again. The effort it took to play into his goddammed VIP delusions! You think the paparazzi would be interested in his ass? Robin Leach wouldn't give him the time of day."

"But his death will bring enough bad publicity to close our doors."

"That bad?"

"Just about."

"Damn."

"Yes. I blame myself. I mean it would be the last straw, but it's been coming. We've been dying a slow death on life support for years."

"But we've been full every winter that I can remember, Oren. Unless there's been a recession or hurricane, I can't remember a winter when we didn't have to hustle around the clock."

Oren went on to explain a sophisticated algorithm of insurance, inflation, competition and ended the soliloquy with "we're broke."

"Then we know what we need to do." Lorna and Oren looked up. They had forgotten that Sharon was still in the room.

"Yes. Call Louis Bodden. Admit defeat."

"No. What we need to do tonight is to get rid of this body, dump the drugs down the toilet, sanitize this room and make it look like Mr Pratt has checked out and left."

"Can I have another cigarette, Lorna?" asked Oren

"Sweet Jesus. What am I supposed to say to the the hotel inspector?" asked Sharon.

15.

"What we need to do now is get him in the trunk of your car and head towards East End."

"My car? Why my car? What if he takes a shit in the back of my Land Rover?" Sharon's mention of Oren's beloved car seemed to have worked better than smelling salts. Oren snapped to attention and was ready to fight to protect the boot of his baby.

"It's the biggest of all our cars. Besides, Pratt liked the finer things in life. If you're depriving him of a hearse and a motorcade we could at least drive him to his final resting place in style."

"And why East?" asked Lorna. "You better not be plannin' to bury the son of a bitch in my back garden."

"Think about it. Current. We can't bury him anywhere on land in the middle of a building boom so he'll have to manage with a naval hero's sendoff. We have to go East and find a spot where we can take advantage of the current. If he's ever seen again will be Jamaica's problem and not ours."

Lorna and Sharon worked in near silence, almost as if they all had previous experience in how to dispose of a dead body and were putting a checklist into action while Oren stood watching in a daze. The late Mr Pratt had left this world in a fetal position and seemed determined to stay that way. Only when Sharon and Lorna decided that it would be necessary to physically manipulate him into a more compact fetal stance was Oren sent out of the room while the other two did what was required.

"Used to be that everybody knew how to lay out the dead. I guess he didn't learn that in university, poor thing," Lorna said. "I sent him downstairs to get a can of condensed milk."

"Remind me again why we're doing this," Sharon said as she pondered the task ahead of them.

"You know as well as me. If the Corniche goes down, you go down and then I'm directly behind you. And the condensed milk is to make sure his duppy follows him out o' here."

"I guess it's nice to hear that we all feel like we're in the same boat," remarked Oren, returning to the room, can in hand.

"I know you're doing this for me. You got your whole life and career ahead of you, Sharon. You could move on to another hotel tomorrow if you wanted to. But me? I ain't got them kinda options. My whole future is tied up in this hotel. If it springs a leak, I sink. And at my age nobody will take me on." Sometimes Lorna despised the Corniche, at the end of days when it hurt to take off her shoes, and longed for a job at a desk. But she didn't know how to do anything at a desk, except clean it. "And me with my police record."

"You've got a record? For what?" asked Sharon.

"Drugs."

"Yeah," snorted Sharon. "Sure."

"No for true. I was busted for that ganja I told you about. Like I said, I was gettin' chemo at the time, but the judge still accepted my guilty plea."

"So you have a drugs charge against your name for medicinal marijuana?"

"Yeah, baby. Times sure changed. But it's there and nobody gon' hire me after a background check. Except for this poor fool." She gestured towards Oren.

"You would never leave me. Would you, Lorna? Even if you had no record..." Oren sounded like a desperate child with abandonment issues. The sound of it snapped them all into the present moment.

"Oren, where the hell would I go?"

"I... I don't know, Lorna. But you've been my right hand all these years. I had to ask. You know what? Ignore me, please. It's been a long day. A long week and I'm stressed. What would I do without you to help me run this place?"

"Lorna runs the place?" asked Sharon, obviously slighted at the conversation. She felt like checking the name tag on her lapel to make sure it still read "Manager" on it.

"You work very hard too, Sharon. All Oren meant is that he and I been working alongside one another for donkey years."

"What I mean," said Oren, "is that Lorna has the business of hotels coursing through her veins. She keeps guest morale high and overheads low."

Sharon could hardly believe what she was hearing. She knew Lorna had been at the hotel longer than any other employee, but surely a housekeeper could be replaced. She was getting increasingly incensed by the familiarity between Lorna and the Corniche's owner. The last twenty-four hours had seemed surreal, even without considering the dead guest.

"She is heavily invested in this establishment," said Oren. "Figuratively and literally."

"You not helping, Bobo," Lorna said with a scowl on her face.

"What am I missing here?" Sharon asked, wide-eyed.

"Lorna is a shareholder."

"What?!"

"Goddammit, Oren." Lorna had gone red in the face.

"A shareholder? Are you fucking kidding me? The maid? The maid owns the hotel? Did one of you slip me drugs? And tell me again why I'm standing here holding a fucking can of condensed milk?"

"Sharon, calm yourself down."

"It's true. Lorna owns one per cent of the Hotel Trust. And if you hold it together long enough to get through this I swear I'll cut you a couple of share certificates too."

"He means it, Sharon. Girl, pull yourself together."

"Listen to me Lorna... I just scraped your last victim up off the floor and I'm in the process of disposing of his body. Please don't tell me to get myself together."

"If we're going to start fighting, could I suggest we turn around, drive into town and turn ourselves in to the police?"

***

Half an hour later Oren was still grumbling from the back seat of his Land Rover while Lorna ignored him from the driver's seat. She was comfortable with the arrangement – if they were stopped by police Oren had instructions to act drunk so it would seem like any other late night during the week when she had to drive him home to Frank Sound to avoid him being breathalysed and arrested.

"God. I can't believe it. A dead body. A dead body in my car. I know I'll have to clean it after this trip. I'll have to wash it inside and out."

"First time for everything," Lorna replied. She knew Oren had never washed a car in his life, his or anyone else's.

"Alright, you two. Enough." Sharon turned to face them both. "We need to be sure what we're going to do, I want a plan in place before we get there so we don't spend more than a few minutes at Pedro. We don't need to speak unless absolutely necessary. Oren, you stand between us and the car and look out for people. Although I doubt that there will be anyone around at this time of night."

"And if they is, they goin' to be up to no good just like us." Sharon was relieved to note that Lorna was slowly returning to her acerbic self, which suggested that the shock of the afternoon might be something that she could recover from.

"Okay. Then what?" asked Oren, who seemed to have difficulty understanding what was to happen next. All night he had stood by in the corner awaiting instructions and direction. It was clear that he didn't cope well in a crisis.

"Well, we grab an end each. Lorna and I, that is. We swing him over the ironshore and into the water."

"Thank you. Thank you both. I'm not lost on how silly this seems, to start talking about employees who go above and beyond the call of duty. So thank you."

"It's the right thing to do," said Sharon flatly. Lorna nodded in agreement.

Sometimes we gotta do what seems like somethin' terrible for the sake o' somethin' right."

*

The Goldberg residence was done up in a monochromatic beige-on-grey style with flecks of the darkly lacquered wood that Sharon had seen in the design and architecture magazines that she loved to stack on her coffee table. It was a style that rich people seemed to love. She had read that it made better backdrops for wealthy families' art collections. She made a mental note to do her next home in the same style, not because she had any art to show off, but because it looked easy to clean and dust wouldn't show up.

"As we used to say as children, it'll take more than one small-teeth comb to sort all this out," said Lorna as she studied a giant, cast-iron frying pan, waiting for it to heat up her secret combination of butter, olive oil and vegetable fat. She fried most breakfast foods with this combination for the flavour it gave: eggs, bacon, tomatoes, green plantain – and she had been pleasantly surprised to find all of these waiting and fresh in Oren's well-appointed kitchen. "Speaking of hair, thank God that styupid gyal you pay for help won't be here today. I wish I understood why you keep her around. If she worked as hard for you as she did lookin' man…"

"She's young, Lorna. And she needed the work."

"And nobody else would give her the time of day. Or work. Same old story."

Oren was happy to see Lorna in his kitchen. She knew it because she had helped him to fit it out. She was the first person to use the percolator carafe, which had been bubbling on the hob and was beginning to fill the room with the aroma of coffee as only Lorna could make it. He knew that she claimed that the secret to her superior coffee was a generous pinch of salt mixed into the ground coffee. He had tried this himself a few times and yet no cup of coffee he had ever attempted himself ever came close to Lorna's.

Sharon watched the two of them with silent fascination. Lorna knew her way around the kitchen. She was realising how obtuse she had been. She'd sometimes noticed the way that Lorna and Oren so casually occupied space together. But now she saw that there was a closeness that she went beyond that, something comfortable about the way they interacted, even when they weren't speaking. They finished each other's sentences. They sat close to one another. How on earth could she never have noticed this? But then, how many times had she ever seen them in close proximity, sitting alone together at the same table or on a shared settee?

"So now you know. I'm having an affair with Hugh," she suddenly blurted out.

"Yes child," said Lorna, in a kind, nurturing voice. "We already covered this."

"And I'm sure we can find a way to keep this off your file with HR," added Oren, patting her hand and smiling.

"But there's more. Much more," she added, looking up.

"Sharon if you tell me you're pregnant for that old married man, I swear I'mma take this skillet breakfast and all and..." Lorna snorted.

"No, no. Nothing like that."

"Then what?"

"Pratt was blackmailing us."

"Well now you can both get back to enjoying yourselves," remarked Oren.

"Well, no. I wish we could. But I can't stop thinking..." her sentence veered off. Oren and Lorna looked up and over, waiting for her to finish her thought.

"Hugh had just written him yet another cheque. If anyone finds it do you think it will look like we... "

"Found it. He had flung it down on the desk with the cash. I tore it up and flushed it down the toilet along with the drugs," said Lorna, turning to face the counter. She popped the toaster down and brought over cups and the carafe, using a tea towel to hold the top as she poured. "I meant to tell you but I was so busy trying to get the place looking like he had checked himself out."

"Thank you, Lorna." Now Sharon was the one who looked close to crying.

"Two cups of this will set us all right."

"I suspect it will take more than coffee for things to feel the same again," said Sharon.

"I did mean to ask. It was made out for a hefty pile of money. You mean to tell me that Sir Hugh was willing to pay that kind of money to keep your affair a secret?"

"Yes. And sometimes it was that much every quarter. I guess it depended on Mr Pratt's other business endeavours and how much champagne he had drunk."

"Fifty grand? To not talk about the two o' you?" Lorna began to shuffle plates of eggs, bacon, tomatoes and plantain over to the table.

"It was so much more than that. He made all these threats. He threatened to expose us, to embarrass us, to ruin us. Well, not so much me but he could have totally ruined Hugh. He had fabricated this ridiculous theory that Hugh had somehow been responsible for his wife's condition. That he had actually done something to put his wife in that coma."

"How do you put someone in a coma?" asked Lorna

"You give them an overdose of insulin. It's happened before. It's hard to diagnose and there was a lot of insulin lying around. Hard not to have it on hand as she was diabetic. Pratt said that the British tabloids would eat up his story and have it in print so fast that his reputation would be ruined before he could bother to sue. He had fabricated some sort of back-up, an evidence or witness. I've forgotten what, but it was enough to scare Hugh." Sharon was relieved to have finally shared this with someone.

"He don't look like the kind of man who would harm anybody to me," said Lorna.

"I'm as sure of that as I can be too. Hugh just isn't capable of something like that. And even if he was he had no reason to share all this with me. I might never have known what Pratt was using it to blackmail him for all that money. I certainly didn't have any contact with the man other than checking him in and out."

Oren sighed. "Pratt really was a piece of work."

"He was a piece o' shit. And gravalicious," said Lorna. "Too damn gravalicious. And by the way. Now you got as much reason as us to keep quiet about all this business. It's us three caught up in it. Four if you count Sir Hugh. And I expect you'd like to stay out of prison long enough to be the next countess."

"Duchess," Sharon corrected. "Now, about those share certificates..."

*

"Are we doing the right thing, Lorna?" The housekeeper thought for a moment as she chewed her lip and navigated yet another roundabout. She was back in the driver's seat. Lorna always enjoyed driving Oren's British SUV. It was an odd month when she didn't find herself behind the wheel shuttling him home to bed when he had overindulged, then on to her own place.

"What we got here is a case of doing the wrong thing for the right reasons, Oren."

"Yeah. I guess you're right. It's also a few minutes too late to second guess." He laughed bitterly.

"Agreed," said Sharon from her spot on the back seat. She had been worried about the practicality of the idea of getting rid of the body, cleaning the room and simply checking Mr Pratt out of the hotel. "Bet you both a beer that nobody will even miss him. Sad. When you think of it he was after all somebody's child."

"He had to be," said Lorna as she shook her head and took another roundabout. "Not to speak bad of the dead but the doctor who delivered that jackass slapped he mama."

16.

To: All
From: Oren Goldberg
Re: Attention to Detail
On my daily rounds, I have been noticing more and more litter about, particularly cigarette butts. Please arrange to keep a tissue or square of paper on you at all times in the event that you might encounter such litter and need a sanitary means of which to pick up, return to your pocket and dispose of later. Let's all do our part!

OG
Oren Goldberg, MBE
President
The Corniche Hotel Trust Ltd.

The departure lounge at Owen Roberts International Airport was an interesting cross-section of Caymanian society if you ignored the tourists returning on the early morning flights to Miami and JFK. There were the fund and company directors who had arrived just twenty-four hours ago for their board meetings and lavish dinners, and were now returning to their offices at law and accountancy firms There was the young socialite, travelling with her mother to treat themselves to breast implants and a facelift (respectively) and then there were the locals. They were leaving for a few days of shopping, or getting off the island until Tropical Storm Lisa had blown out of the region. Shell-shocked from the last bad storm just a decade past, they were all too happy to shut up their homes to escape having to sit through another such event. The last one had left Sharon's father on antidepressants for months, even after the roof had been fixed and new grass had been shipped in bales and rolled onto the naked earth.

"But that couldn't possibly be the Jennets over there," said Sharon's mother.

"Where?"

"Coming out of security now. Isn't that old man Jennet?"

"It sure is," answered her husband, thankful for the recent cataract surgery that had restored his eyesight to nearly perfect. "And boy, he's a old man now. Sand crab done diggin' his grave."

"Who you callin' old man? She looks good. And she's older than me."

"You'd look good too if you never struck a lick in all your days." Mrs Phelan shushed her husband as Mr Jennet approached in a wheelchair pushed by a conservatively dressed caregiver, with his wife walking at his side. The two couples exchanged greetings and made themselves comfortable in the departure lounge.

Mrs Phelan and Mrs Jennet looked knowingly at one another and managed unconvincing smiles. They had been sitting together for several minutes, and the four had paired off into two conversations. The men were complaining about traffic and lamenting the sad reality that you can no longer sleep in Cayman with your door unlocked, while the wives were dancing around the issue of their cultural shellshock. *Please don't mention hurricanes*, thought Sharon's mother to herself. *Please, God. Can we get out of here without talking about the "H" word, or that name that starts with an "I".*

"It's funny, isn't it? I remember such hardship. No apples till Christmas. Clothes made from potato sacks, smokepots and swarms of mosquitoes that could suck the blood out of a cow in a couple of minutes. But I'd happily return to that."

"Me too," agreed Mrs Jennet. "But all the antidepressants on this island wouldn't keep me here for another big storm."

"Have you looked around? We're not the only ones. Both women looked up and pivoted their heads around the departure lounge, recognizing the room full of familiar faces escaping for a weekend of shopping in Miami, Fort Lauderdale and Tampa.

"My grandmother used to talk about the effects of '32. It sounded like an epidemic of depression and anxiety. History repeats itself." Mrs Jennet looked grim.

"And guilt. I feel guilty complaining. People don't die here when a storm hits and I don't feel right complaining about the grass that got ripped outta the ground or the roof that needs repairs, but it's a terrible experience all the same."

The other lady could only agree. You had to have been there to understand. "I know we got it good. I try to think of Jamaica and Haiti and BVI."

"You can say that again."

"Is your daughter still away studying?"

"No. No, she's been back for some time. She's the manager at the Corniche."

"It's nice to hear that somebody's children have come back. And in tourism. I'm glad to hear it. Does she enjoy the work?"

"So far. You're right, though. None of that generation went into tourism, did they? Hedge funds and high finance were more attractive, I guess." The gate agent appealed for passengers needing special assistance to prepare to board.

Mrs Phelan paused, worried for a second that the other woman might know something about Sharon and the Englishman, that she was about to let the secret out and then all hell would break loose. Sooner or later she might have to come clean with her husband about Sharon's secret relationship. But hopefully it wasn't going to happen today in the departure lounge of Owen Roberts International Airport. If there had to be a confrontation she hoped that it would happen in the privacy of their home. Hopefully this love affair, as Sharon kept calling it, would run its course and the secret might never need disclosing at all.

What Sharon was thinking, getting involved with an older, white, English aristocrat was beyond her understanding. Honestly. There were some very nice young boys at their church looking for good wives. Granted, whoever ended up marrying Sharon would need a good helper five days a week who could cook, clean and iron. Sharon couldn't boil water and had never learned to iron anything other than her hair. The girl was naïve and self-involved. But then again she was booksmart and big-hearted.

"Yes, yes. Nice to see all the young people coming back with medical degrees and such. For years it felt like everybody's child was either studying accounting or law. Things sure have changed." The other woman stared into space, her eyes seeming to look for some landmark that no longer existed.

Mrs Phelan unclenched her toes and relaxed. Sharon had a lot to answer for, causing her this stress. Surely the girl had encountered enough married old businessmen travelling solo who checked into the Corniche to know better than to throw herself at this one.

"They sure have. I remember the first terminal on this site. It wasn't much more than a shack."

"Yes! I'd forgotten about that. We couldn't travel or pick someone up without stopping for hamburgers. I don't think I've had a hamburger that good since."

Mrs Phelan had to remind herself that the island had evolved and with a population this large, gossip wouldn't be as widely spread as it had once been. This was still on her mind when the other couple and their employee departed to take advantage of early boarding. Less than a minute later her husband returned to the seat next to her, looking displeased, and carrying a rum cake.

"I don't know why you entertain that woman for so long," he said. He was supposed to be watching what he ate and would swear high and low that the cake was a gift for someone in Miami but would probably end up eating the whole thing by himself. "A gossip of the lower order. I heard her trying to suss out news about Sharon and I had to get up and leave. She tell you their youngest daughter shacked up with another woman? I bet not."

"Hush, nuh? You got half o' Cayman reading your lips. She was as useful to me as I was to her. I told her just what I wanted her to know."

"Conniving of you," said Mr Phelan lovingly. "You know she gone to choir practice with every last detail you told her."

"Let's go. They're boarding," said Mrs Phelan as she gathered her belongings and her thoughts.

No one, least of all the Jennets or Phelans, noticed the last glamorous passenger to join the queue behind them to board the 737 and take her place discreetly in seat 1A. If Sharon had been on this shopping trip, she would immediately have recognized Ms Davis.

17.

"So sorry that we're about to miss our regular visit to the Corniche. It's our fave place to be when we run away from home. But I had to post this/shout out to mention their stellar customer service. When I tuned into the Weather Network this morning and realized that Hurricane Lisa was going to throw a spanner into our plans, I immediately phoned them. Sharon, the manager personally got on the line, cancelled our reservation and refunded our credit card payment without penalty. She also promised to personally call to let us know when they would be ready for guests again after the storm. Now that's someplace I will be returning to indefinitely! " –GwenA, Nova Scotia

"Why didn't you ever tell me?"

"About what?"

"You know, about what. I mean, we're close, aren't we? And I told you about Hugh and I."

"Chile, I knew about you and Hugh long before you told me. You glow like a Christmas tree when the two o' you near each other."

"Oh you mean like you and Mr Oren?"

"That is entirely different, Sharon. Oren is my boss. He and I have never had that kind of thing goin'..."

"Okay, not quite the same, but I can't imagine how I never noticed that the two of you are so close."

"We are good friends."

"And I always took you for such a loner. Certainly not one to have such close friends."

"What surprises you? The fact that I have close friends, or that the maid could have important friends?"

"Actually it wasn't that I wanted to ask you about. It's your other secrets I was asking about."

"My tattoos?"

"Your shares in the Corniche. Why do you keep working so hard if you're...you know...rich."

"The only dividend them shares have ever paid are some job security and a little personal satisfaction when people are rude to me."

"What do you mean?"

"I mean when people come here on maxed-out credit cards and think it's okay to talk down to me. You know the type. I do my bow, I call them sir and madam, and I smile to myself."

"Because you own a little piece of the place?"

"Because I own a little piece of the beach. It's a little piece of hope. Those three shares mean plenty more than money to me. They're a slice of hope. Retirement, maybe no student loans for my grandchildren. They might never mean a payout, but they mean that I'm one of the few Caymanians who still own a few grains of this beach."

"So you don't think you'll see heaps of cash someday soon?"

"It ain't that simple, Sharon. It means that a piece of what my great-grandfather sold off for pennies and pounds got returned to me. In their day, Seven Mile Beach was worthless. You could hardly even call it real estate. Nobody wanted to live here. It was worth less than swamp. You couldn't predict a storm and you couldn't build anything that could stand up to a storm anyway."

"It's not like you're doing badly. You've got that nice house. And you've got a good job. A good life, too."

"How many maids you know? How many locals are left that work these jobs? I had some hard luck and I made some bad decisions, and my only advantage in life so far was inheriting my Mama's house and land without a mortgage."

"Go on."

"Me. Me who had so little now actually owns this tiny little piece of something that so few people can claim ownership in."

"So why is it a secret?"

"Of course it's a secret, Sharon. Look at me again. I'm the maid. Those three shares are the only thing all these years that I got that makes me feel special. Why should I have to tell anyone?"

"So if I get a couple of shares in the trust do I have to do the same thing?"

"You can do whatever you like. You can go upstairs to the top floor and scream off the balcony that you own the place. But you'll look like a damn fool, or a madwoman. And it will get you a lot of the wrong kind of attention."

"You're right, I suppose."

"And honestly, Sharon. What would be the point of talking about all this? It don't make me no different. It certainly don't mean I'm any richer. All it has ever meant was something to go home to and think about at night that made me smile before I went to sleep."

"Woah," said Sharon. "Wait a second. You think about your stocks and bonds in bed at night? That's creepy, Lorna. You need to get yourself a man. Or a starter cat."

"Damn fool. I need a cat about as bad as I need a man. Both do the hell they like and neither give you what you need."

"A bit of companionship might be good for you. And you never know, you might fall in love. Or get married."

"Now you talkin' like a madwoman."

Lorna was a tough nut to crack. Once you cracked the surface, she was a loyal and funny ally and friend. But she was still, and probably always would be, caustic.

"I think I'm beginning to understand. It makes you feel special."

"Yes. It makes me feel special. This was all land that our great-grandparents sold for shillings. You couldn't grow anything on it and it wasn't safe to build houses on. You only knew a hurricane was coming when the barometer started to fall."

"Speaking of hurricanes, what do you make of this weather? A good blow would ruin us for the season. Forever, maybe."

"Yeah, you can say that again. And poor Oren is having kittens. It couldn't be at a worse time."

"I can't understand how things could have gotten so bad at the Corniche. I mean, people have been flocking here for the past half a century and paying top dollar for the honour."

"Things have changed. Times have changed. And hotels have changed most of all. But the truth is, this place been real good to us all."

"Yeah, I guess."

"Sharon, would you explain to me how it was you could afford to go abroad to study, not once, not twice but three times?"

"I was here on work experience. They saw my potential."

"They?"

"The Corniche Hotel Trust."

"You mean the Goldbergs."

"No. I mean yes. I mean, it was a bursary from the parent company of the hotel."

"No, you silly, stupid girl. It was not."

"Then who signed off on it?"

"Oren. Didn't I just say that?"

"Well of course, Lorna. I mean, I'm sure that Oren had a lot to do with it."

"No, Sharon. Oren did it."

"What? What do you mean? And why are we talking about this now?"

"Listen to me, Sharon. Listen to me very carefully, not only because it's important but because you should know this."

Sharon stared Lorna down. "Continue."

"Percy was the worst concierge on the planet. He worked here because he couldn't get no job no place else. He was useless. He dropped shit. Usually when guests was looking and it was usually expensive and usually something belonging to the guests."

"I don't follow."

"Patience, Sharon. You will. Then there's me. My first mammogram ten years ago happened because I had better health insurance than some of the bankers who have lunch here. That was followed by a biopsy and then a lumpectomy. Then there was radiation. All of this happened while I was on paid leave. All of this was paid for. You following me?"

"Yes, Lorna. We have good jobs. This is a nice place to work."

"Yes. And sickness comes on horseback and leaves on snail. Last but not least, there's you, Sharon."

"Me?"

"You."

"Go on. I guess it's too much to ask you to lay off the cigarettes. The smoke is killing me."

Lorna lit another menthol. "Now listen. One day about twenty years ago your mama came here to this very hotel and asked to talk to me. It was an October afternoon like the one we had today. She was upset. She said she needed to talk to me and it was urgent, so I took her to the dining room and sat her down at that table at the end, and the first thing she did was lean forward and start to cry."

"What was wrong with her?"

"What was wrong with her was you, fool."

"Me?"

"You."

"She had come home and found the house smelling of ganja. She sat down and started tellin' me all this. We'd been sitting at another table writing cheques when your mother came in and started to cry. And man could your mother cry. There was no hiding it. Wailing like a banshee. So Oren got up, sent for some tea and came and sat down next to her. He took her hand. She was crying so hard I was worried she might need to blow her nose with the corner of the tablecloth,"

"She was crying because of me?"

"Yeah. She had followed the smell like a dog at the airport to find a pound of weed hidden in your bedroom. I can't believe you were naïve enough to think your mama and I don't know what weed smells like. She flushed it down the toilet then drove straight here. She was in a state that day. She was frightened you would end up in court for drugs. A whole lot worse than getting knocked up at seventeen like her and me."

"I remember, like it was yesterday. It wasn't even my marijuana. It belonged to a boy I'd been seeing. I've lost touch with him. I wonder where he lives now... " Sharon lost eye contact with Lorna as she searched her memory for the boy's face and last known address.

"HMP Northward," said Lorna. "So Oren and I calmed your mummy down while she told us that you was looking to repeat history, going no place fast. It was Oren who came up with the idea. He said it sounded like you had too much time on your hands and what you needed was something to replace this boy. A challenge. A rewarding challenge."

"So that's how I ended up here?" Sharon asked. "On work experience?"

"You don't know what that took, to make it look like you warranted it. You were the first student to go through the hotel's apprenticeship and scholarship scheme. We didn't even have one until that week."

"The scholarship was started for me?"

"Yes, chile. You was the first. At the time it went by another name. We called it *Everybody's bonuses.*"

"I think I know where this is going," said Sharon.

"Well I should hope so. 'Cause I'll tell you where this all came from. We made it, we did it, we bankrolled it all for the love of your mama. We made opportunities for you like no one had seen before, and before the big hotels started doing it to make themselves look good. You know why we always double up on work around here? Because we worked so hard those years that we still ain't used to getting much sleep. To this day I can get a night's sleep kotched up in a chair and then do another shift. Your generation would call the labour board if you had to work the way we did."

"Okay, fine. You've made your point and sent me on a guilt trip. Especially now that you're both turning a blind eye to my relationship with Hugh."

"What you suppose we been doin' all this time?" They were sitting there in Miss Lorna's car, staring to the west, out to sea, as they made no rush to finish their supersized milkshakes.

They rarely ate outdoors at this time of the day, not even this time of year when it began to get noticeably milder. Lunch had felt like a special event, despite being ordered from the drive-thru. It was uncommonly mild, thanks to the nearby storm system. The water along Seven Mile Beach was calm but moody in colour; by contrast the sky looked tempestuous and there wasn't a bird or insect in Lorna's peripheral vision. This had her feeling uneasy, even though she knew that according to the meteorologists, they were out of the woods. But Lorna knew better than to turn her back on the dormant potential of the Cayman Trench. This was why her ancestors had always thought better than to build here, even along the leeward side of the island.

"What's he like?" she asked, starting the car.

"What's who like? Father Christmas?"

"You know who I mean."

"You've known him just as long as I have.".

"Yes, but I don't know him."

"Are you asking what I think you're asking?"

"No chile. I don't need to know about that. Nobody don't need to know about that."

"He's exactly the same as the Hugh that you know, to be honest. There aren't two of him." She bit her lip as she thought of an example. "You know he takes a whole lot of showers and baths."

"You're talking to the person who brings the towels and robes. And he goes through nearly as many of them as Pratt."

"For an entirely different reason. He needs a lot of hot showers and baths with mineral salts. That's why he loves our bathtubs so much."

"That's lovely, Sharon. So the man is real clean... "

"And he sings."

"He sings?"

"Yes. He sings a lot. He has a terrific memory and he knows all these songs, you know? So he sings in the bath. In the shower."

"My, sweet," Lorna said, not sounding nearly as sarcastic as Sharon would have expected.

"Yes. Yes, it is. He's always singing me show tunes from the bathroom."

"Say what?"

"Well, not just show tunes. He does some great renditions of Elton John. And Neil Diamond."

"That sounds real sweet. Real, real sweet. I didn't realize he was so light in the heels but if it makes you happy, Sharon..."

"He has a beautiful voice,"

"Oh, I bet he does. You and your GBF got a favourite musical?"

"You look a little green, Lorna.. I think you might be jealous that no one has ever sung 'On the Street Where You Live', or 'Something Good', to you."

"Oh, so romantic."

"While we're in the bath together. While he rubs my feet."

"Yeah, girl. I'm real jealous."

"I see that. You're turning full-on green, you know."

"It's nausea."

Miss Lorna turned right at the Seven Mile Beach road, slowly making her way in the traffic to return them to work.

"What do you think is going to happen? To the Corniche, I mean?" asked Sharon.

"So much of that depends on Oren, I suppose. I love the man like cook-food. He's practically family, but when it comes to business he sure ain't his father."

"You mean Oren's father was a better hotelier?"

"I hate to say it, but yes. The man was a bastard and a human rights violation but when it came to business, he was a force not to be questioned."

"Did you know him well?"

"Nobody could really have known old Mr Goldberg well. Not even his wife I think."

"I don't follow... "

"Oren takes after her more. She was real kind, Missy Goldberg."

"They were that different?

"Yes. He was a real bastard. The son of a bitch worked you hard, paid you shit and replaced you without a second thought if you fell behind. She was an angel."

"And the Corniche turned a profit."

"A profit? Boy, that was a golden age for real. The Corniche was a goldmine. Old Man Goldberg went to work every day till his last. Keeled over and died in his desk chair."

"Things have changed."

"Yeah. Oren is real kind and thoughtful. He's a wonderful man. And a terrible businessman. He's good to his people. No turnover to speak of, and a steady decline in business. Ain't his fault. He wanted to be a artist. Or make documentary films, or save the reefs and rainforests."

"Couldn't he have found a balance between the two?"

"It's hard. Old Man was what they call a visionary in those interviews you see with business tycoons on TV. A businessman like I've never seen before or since. But Jesus Christ, the man could be rude to royalty. And he was, more than once in my memory."

"There's got to be a balance in this business. Surely we should be able to run this outfit and retain good people while still manage to profit. But hearing all this makes me understand why you go out of your way to help Oren, why you'd do almost anything to get him out of hot water."

"Maybe I'm more like the father than the son."

"Maybe." She looked over at Lorna. "You're hard as nails. But I suspect you're motivated by love as well."

"Oh Christ, Sharon. I don't love the man."

"I suspect you do. I'm not sure how you love him, but I'm sure you do. There's plenty types of love, you know. No, hear me out." Lorna had opened her mouth after a sharp intake of breath and Sharon knew that she had to get her point over before she got her razor blade tongue into gear. "After all, those shares don't pay a dividend. You might never get to reap the rewards.

"Not yet, but I could end up wealthy one day. You done matchmakin'? I need to get back to work."

"Or just about as wealthy as a typical retired hotel maid on a pension. Just think about it before you answer. You're not getting any younger. Either of you."

***

There is no substitute for hard work. These were the words on the little plaque next to Mr Smythe's laptop on the desk. Should have had that tattooed on my bunkey years ago, Lorna thought to herself as she tidied the already pristine room. A life of missed opportunities was her lot. If it was raining soup outside, life would find her standing there with only a fork. She was still in the room, feeling sorry for herself when the guest returned.

"Just the lady I wanted to see. How are ya?"

"Not bad, Miss Ruby. How's you?"

Ruby Smythe took both of Lorna's hands in her own, the way that she always had when the older woman wanted her to stop and have an intimate chat. The two sat down. It wasn't something that Lorna would ever have done with most guests, but it would have been rude to decline the welcome few minutes off her feet so she allowed herself to get caught up with her old friend.

"How are things, Lorna?"

"Oh fine. Just fine."

"No, seriously. Lee's worried. He says the hotel is too empty, even for this time of year."

"Well, you know. It was a slow summer. But we managed."

"Poor Oren," said Mrs Smythe, staring into space. 'He's twice as nice as his father, but half the businessman. Lee and I worry about him. Whenever we speak he sounds like he's on the brink of breaking. We worry about all of you. I'm glad you're sure that everything's hunky-dory."

"Tha's real sweet, Miss Ruby. But you don't need worry. If there's one thing I got faith in it's this place. We managed this long. We gon' get by."

"Then we won't worry."

"Not on your nice vacation. Not when you come all this way and your plans lookin' to get ruined with this storm comin'."

"Oh yeah," the guest answered absently. "I guess we should start thinking about packing up our toys and making our way to higher ground. Metaphorically speaking."

"You got your plans made?"

"Oh yes, dearie. We're flying out some time tomorrow afternoon. Oren invited us to stay at the house, but we think it's best we get home."

"Well if you got that all looked after, I gon' come by after you had yuh breakfast and help you get packed up."

"Oh, that would be so nice, Lorna. The later the better. Lee needs a kick in the pants for breakfast now that he's old. Sometimes I wish I could take you home with us. I wish I had somebody like you to get me organized. Nobody sorts a closet or packs a suitcase like you."

"Me? What could I do?"

"Oh my God, Lorna. You have such a talent for organizing and managing and planning... well... everything. And you don't even know it."

"Talent, Miss Ruby? Me?" Lorna looked at the guest skeptically.

"I predict your next career, you'll be a professional organizer."

"A what? You mean people make money for that?"

"C'mere," said the guest as she led Lorna to the closet. "I wanna show you something."

Mrs Smythe flung open the closet door with a dramatic flourish. "See what you did here? Incredible work."

"Hangin' up clothes?"

"No, Lorna. Much more than that. You sorted all of my outfits for this trip into day and night. Surely you must've known what you were doing?" The guest's eyes widened as Lorna shook her head, bashfully.

"I appreciate it, Miss Ruby, but all I done was hang up the clothes you brought and put the darks on the left and the lights and whites on the right."

"You mean to tell me you didn't even know you were sorting them into day and night? Amazing."

By the time Lorna had left the Smythes' room she was beaming from the compliments, though she still wasn't entirely convinced that she had done anything that had required any skill or talent. She also hadn't realized that there were people who got paid to do this sort of thing. A professional organizer. Who even knew? Maybe that was something that she could do on the side, like a freelance thing.

However, by the time the lift had touched down and the doors opened to deposit her at the lobby, Lorna had come to the conclusion that the entire conversation, the whole experience had been no more than Mrs Smythe being nice to her and looking for a way to brighten her day. Which it had done for a moment. After all, Lorna had never been anything other than the maid and that was all she would ever be. But it had been an unfamiliar sensation to feel special. It had been nice to feel for a moment as though she had the potential to do something more with her life than clean.

18.

The Corniche Hotel
Seven Mile Beach Grand Cayman

Dear Louis,

Thank you for your kind consideration in sharing your thoughts on the future of the Corniche. A few of my thoughts following our lovely luncheon are below. Sorry I had to dash!

I think that somehow doubling the C's room capacity is a no-go for several reasons, not least of all being that this would utterly ruin the boutique-hotel vibe that we are so renowned for. A ten-story, 200 room hotel just isn't as relaxing as we are. It simply doesn't matter about the colour palette, aromatherapy candles, spa services, soap concierge that would come with a larger building, because something would be lost. It would be an entirely different animal altogether.

You're right, of course about evolving interior design trends. I am hopeful that this recent trend in ripping out rare materials and crown mouldings and replacing them with mid-century modern Corbusier and Mies Van der Rohe knockoffs has died and bled from the zeitgeist of contemporary hotel design. The rest of us (i.e. the custodians of grande-dame maximalist design and above all – comfort and luxury) can rest easy now. I would rather sell now, lock, stock and wine cellar than see my parents' dream of a comfortable, casual yet glamorous and elegant hotel in the old beach club style, be lost or tampered with.

While the C was initially designed and outfitted along the design ethos of the Hollywood Regency style (although my mother often referred to it with the earlier terminology of Regency Moderne) with the palette of colours that would evoke this part of the world (variations upon celadon, robin's egg, sand and sisal), it might be time to consider a refresh. The dining room, champagne bar, pool bar especially are beginning to look a little dated, evoking memories of abandoned Giorgio perfume boxes and Rodeo Drive awnings. Can we talk again about sourcing some of those Bengali design fixtures and stuffed tigers?

Now to the sad topic of sale. While it was not really on my mind when we initially sat down to lunch, the estimates that you provided out of thin air have certainly piqued my interest. As you know, the local beneficial ownership laws protect the privacy of the other shareowners of the trust and I would have to consult them on even considering a sale while respecting their anonymity. From my own point of view, I would certainly consider selling if these numbers are realistic with all these zeroes... albeit regretfully. If that sultan you were at college with, or that Chinese group building the new cruise ship terminal are genuinely interested, then by all means, do set up a meeting. I'm happy to agree to your 3% if these people are going to be generous with the zeroes.

Thanks. Again. Lunch on me next time, as soon as all this storm madness has passed? I suspect you're off to Miami like everyone else.

OG
Oren Goldberg, MBE
President
The Corniche Hotel Trust Ltd.

The Goldberg residence off Frank Sound Road was spectacular. Yes, that was the correct word, thought Miss Lorna. No more, no less. It reminded her of a house in a movie, but she could never quite figure out which one. It was somewhere, there in the back of her subconscious. *The Remains of the Day*? *Rebecca*? *Something's Gotta Give*? She really did watch too much TV late at night.

Ultimately there were aspects of all the houses in all the movies and shows that she was reminded of when she visited Old Man Goldberg's house. Maybe there was a touch of madness here too, like in *The Cat & the Canary*.

If this place was mine I'd have given it a name by now, she thought as she turned into the driveway past the double gates that were always open. *But something made up and not from no book. Wouldn't want it burning to the ground.*

How many houses had gates that welcomed her with open doors and open arms, much less one that she possessed a set of keys for? What she always studied going up the long, tree-lined drive, and the casual visitor wouldn't notice, was the landscaping. There were enough fruit trees, edible shrubs and plants on the parcel to feed the family for a few weeks if Armageddon came along.

Old Man Goldberg had been an eccentric character. The trees were all planted with a purpose in mind and that purpose was survival. With the exception of a little croton here and there, probably planted for colour (and to scare away the duppies) there was nothing that couldn't be consumed. Coconuts, limes, oranges (both the local and Seville variety), bamboo and banana suckers were everywhere. A mature tamarind and guinep tree punctuated the house like a pair of reading glasses. Under each tree sat succulents; on closer inspection you could find aloe vera or some other edible plant, placed just so to insulate the roots and take advantage of the shade.

At the entrance, grand, intricately carved wooden doors (hand-carved, finished and varnished then shipped from somewhere in Central America) introduced the visitor to the repeating motif of palm fronds, ferns, bay leaves and cloves that carried over into everything from the carpet runners to the wallpaper. Lorna assumed that this meant that all of these had been designed, built and made for the house, not because she knew anything about this sort of business, but because it made more sense to design and make it than to go out and look for it or put it on a shopping list. Be on the lookout for palm fronds and bay leaves and flowers, preferably in blue and white or eau-de-nil.

Sometimes when she was stocking the pantry or freezer, or after putting Oren to bed, Lorna liked to pretend that this was her house, her double front doors and double glass fridges, chandeliers that she had chosen herself (dishwasher-safe of course – even with a mansion like this she was still Lorna Paige Ebanks) and of course, her staircase. With Oren left fast asleep on his stomach so that she didn't have to worry about him choking on his own vomit while she was daydreaming, she would descend the staircase imagining herself in expensive shoes that were as beautiful as they were uncomfortable. And shoulder pads, like in an episode of *Dynasty*. She was Linda Evans. No, screw that. She was Joan Goddamned Collins. Fuck that too. She was Alexis "Queen of the Bitches" Colby. But she always made the mistake of looking over at the polished, curving handrail and saw her own dark, spotted and aged hands, cracked from years of polish and disinfectant. No amount of Dead Sea hand cream (guest bath vanity) or Huskers Lotion could fix that. By the time she was at the bottom of the stairs and one of those uncomfortable stiletto heels was leaving the step for the marble tile, she was once again good ole Lorna. Staid, dependable and allergic to change.

Her phone rang, interrupting her daydreams It was Sharon. Of course it was. It was always Sharon.

"What up, girl?"

"I just wanted to make sure that it's still okay invite to invite Hugh to stay at Oren's while the storm passes."

"Okay."

"Well? Is it still okay?"

"Nothin' changed since the last we spoke and I told you to invite him. He either needs someplace to stay or you need to get his ass on a plane outta here."

"He'll probably accept. Just so you know," answered Sharon tentatively.

"Ain't that the intention for invitin' him?"

"If he does accept, it's gonna mean kind of a big deal. Like us coming out, sort of."

"Well Sharon, you about to shack up with the man. Not me."

"It's just a big milestone. I'm preparing myself. We're moving from one kind of relationship to another. It's all happening pretty fast."

"I don't see why you sound so nervous. He yuh man, ain't he?"

"Oh, Lorna. It's not like that. I mean, we're graduating from a love affair to a real, honest-to-god, grown-up relationship. Don't you think? Until now it's just been...a...a... "

"Bonin'?"

"Lorna. You know we were never just boning. What Hugh and I have is a..."

"Suh hep muh Crise, Sharon. If I hear you say love affair one more goddamn time, I swear I gon' vomit. Hugh ain't no Warren Beatty and you sure as hell ain't Annette Benin.'"

"I just know that people are going to judge us when they find out. They'll talk and they'll judge me, on so many levels."

"Listen. The two o' you's grown adults. If you and Hugh want to swing off the rafters, it ain't nobody' business but yours. Jus' keep the noise down." This made Sharon giggle.

"I doubt that will ever happen. Not with the state of Hugh's joints. Okay. I'll ask him. Anything else?"

"Yeah. Lock the door."

"Okay. I'll let you know what he says. About staying with us, I mean. Not about locking doors. You all done up there? I'll be coming up for lunch with Hugh, if you need any help."

"No, no. I'm good." Lorna appreciated the offer, but she could get more done on her own. She was also enjoying the quiet solitude.

"What about you?"

"What about me?"

"I mean your house. Have you seen to your own house and garden? You sure have spent a lot of time getting Oren's house ready for all of us."

"Not so much, come to think of it."

"Not so much?"

"I don't got nuthin' expensive to lock up or secure. Jut the ol' house and garden. They's accordion shutters on the windows. And if the storm is a direct hit I gone have to plant every blessed thing in the garden anyway. Why you ask?"

"Umm, does the concept of putting your own mask on first mean anything to you?"

"No. I didn't make no plans to go Miami. I catch you later, okay?"

***

Over many years Lorna had come to love the Goldberg house almost as much as she adored her own little cottage. Her attachment didn't have all that much to do with its size, grandeur and luxury, although she would happily move in tomorrow if invited. All around her were mementoes, photographs, and reminders of happy times, connections, relationships and members of Oren's family.

Today Oren was miles away at the Corniche. Usually, she would take her time with her visits to the house to replenish supplies, and often just sit in a room and imagine that this was her home, this was her life, and these pictures were her kinfolk. But there was no more time for playing lady of the house today. She was repressing a bad feeling about Tropical Storm Lisa and wanted the pantry and supplies to be prepared for a direct hit.

Some people scramble like headless chickens in a casino when a hurricane or tropical storm is approaching. A few others are so prepared that they begin hurricane season by turning over packages of survivalist food stashes and checking the expiry dates, buying an extra case of bottled water and UHT milk and then returning to life as usual. Miss Lorna was in the latter category. Preparation for survival was built into her Caymanian DNA. She could check the dates, visit the barometer to note the fall, and dump a couple of chlorine dioxide tablets into the cistern without a lull in the conversation; if you were on the phone with her you would swear she was in her chair with her feet up crocheting. At any given time she knew that she was ready for three houseguests at her own home and at least another fifteen at Oren's. She preferred to pass the time during a storm at Oren's, not because of the company but because there was that diesel generator out back, which meant that she could watch a half a dozen DVD's and then go out to begin to clean up the damage, if there was any.

Bottled water? Cases stacked in the pantry and another column in the garage – enough for months. Tinned Jamaican cheese was also stacked high, with several large bags of hardtack leaning against the plinth. Next were more stacks of tinned tuna, salmon, peaches, pears and sweetened condensed milk, although she had totally gone off this product recently and wasn't entirely sure why. Oh wait. Yes she did.

Freeze-dried ice cream sandwiches in sealed pouches, the kind they ate in space, were at the ready. New board games were on the shelf, as well as several jigsaw puzzles in case the power and generator both failed. She even had Oren's prescriptions filled and reserves at the ready, although what he thought he was going to do with that much Viagra in the house she dared never ask.

"And hand sanitizer," said the driver of the wholesale distributor's van, as if he had read Miss Lorna's mind. "Plenty, plenty o' hand sanitizer."

"God only knows what them people plan to do with that much toilet paper," he said to his colleague in the passenger seat when the door had closed and he was ready to reverse and make his way back West. The woman had received the delivery, signed the chit and not taken her hawk-like eyes off them until they turned out the gate.

"The lady of the house?" asked the man in the left-hand seat.

"Anybody who can afford this house can afford a friendlier side-piece than that."

19.

"Cayman Battens Hatches as Lisa Approaches"

"Iguana Culler Accidentally Shot in Buttock with Pellet Gun"

"Stayover Tourists Urged to make Travel Arrangements"

"Combination Chicken/Ostrich Farm Denied Planning Permission"

Sharon and Hugh were waiting for their orders at one of the shacks along the road that followed the coast of East End that served fried fish to order. There was a deceptive calm everywhere. It betrayed the turmoil and destruction that could be on the way. The sea was as flat as a pane of glass and there was no sign of so much as a faint breeze from the east as Sharon sat, enjoying her time alone with Hugh despite the heat and humidity.

Sharon remembered her retreat to Miami, well before the last storm to hit Cayman arrived – she was glad not to have been present. It was noted as one of the worst in history and she had been shocked on her return two weeks later, when the runway was sufficiently dried out, to find that she didn't recognize the island. Buildings had been obliterated from the landscape along with vegetation and landscaping. For months she had found herself momentarily lost in the car on roads that she had known her entire life. Roads without their signs and wayfinding landmarks were foreign lands. She tried to put the possibility that this was about to happen again out of her mind.

"I can't believe that you ordered the barracuda. Brave man. My grandmother used to tell me that if you got one that was poisoned your teeth would fall out."

"We could just get on a plane and go to Miami or Fort Lauderdale."

"It's far too late for that. And we'd risk running into my parents, or a member of my big-mouthed family or someone else who knows us."

"Oh, I see."

"Yes. And I'm not quite ready for my folks to have to acknowledge us publicly yet. My mother is being surprisingly quiet lately and I'd like that to go on for as long as possible. I suspect this will mean a presentation at court or an MBE or something."

"Sharon, darling. Florida's a pretty big place."

"Yeah, but our airport isn't. And Florida is full of Caymanians. Years ago, my father was spotted at a strip club during a bachelor party in Miami. It wasn't even his party. My mother was notified of the news by phone before he had even left."

"Oh my."

"Yeah. Unless you're gonna charter a plane just for the two of us, flying out at this late hour just isn't an option for us." Hugh began to scroll through the contacts on his phone.

"Well it is a little last-minute, but if you think it's for the best and if you'd feel more comfortable... "

"Oh how sweet are you?" Sharon said, as she covered the screen of his smartphone with her hand. But she was touched that Hugh would consider going to the trouble and expense, to go to such measures just for her.

"There is another option."

"Hmm? What's that?"

"You stay here. With me."

"Where?"

"With my friends."

"By friends, do you mean your Mr Goldberg and Miss Lorna?"

"Yes. Would that make you uncomfortable?"

"No, not in the least. What about you? Same question."

"Could it be arranged?"

"We've already been invited to stay. I would just need to call and accept then buy some spirits so we don't show up empty-handed. That would be truly unacceptable."

"More unacceptable than you showing up to a sleepover at your boss's house with your older married side-piece?"

"Where did even you learn that word, Hugh?" asked Sharon, feigning shock and disapproval. "You are not nor have you ever been my side-piece."

"Not even for a month or two in the beginning?"

"Not even in your imagination."

Sharon hadn't had much time with Hugh since the night when they had disposed of Pratt. The night, as they now called it. She hadn't been able to bring him up to date, even with a heavily redacted and sanitized version of the events that took place behind the room door and over the cliffs at Pedro. She never would be able to tell him, but she did need to sit down and explain to him in somewhat greater detail why it was now acceptable for them to come out of the closet and be seen together, at least in some circles.

"So," he added. "Does that mean it's finally okay to at least come clean with your family and friends?"

"I'm sorry that all this has seemed so sordid. When it's not. I still don't know how I feel that you've somehow learned what a side-piece is. But, yes. Let's start by testing the waters with my friends from work before we face the Phelan clan. Besides, I need to be here to get to the Corniche as soon as the danger has passed. And someone will need to check on my parents' house and see to the damage."

"There's also our little condo on the beach. We shall need to get there quickly too."

"Yes. It feels funny having to worry about damage before we've even moved in. I haven't even thought about it. I haven't even thanked you properly."

"There's no need to thank me, my darling. It's your home. Our home."

"I can't wait," she said and touched his shoulder for as long as it felt safe.

20.

"...Islands Preparing for Direct Hit..."

"Cast of Reality TV Series Stranded in Caymans"

"Should Government House be Moved from SMB?"

"Whe' you been?" Sharon hated it when Lorna or anyone else did seemed to be keeping tabs on her. She was waiting just outside the side entrance to the Corniche, and had obviously been poking her head out the door every few minutes.

"I needed an extended lunch with Hugh. He says he can tell I'm stressed and wants to stick around a few more days for support. If only he knew my level of stress and why."

"Boy, I glad you got a shoulder to lean on today. I hope you took your blood pressure pills with lunch. Come with me."

Lorna led her to a quiet corner outside and just past the double doors, which wasn't difficult. The Corniche was as deserted as the rest of Seven Mile Beach. Several flights were being added to the schedule at the airport and anyone who hadn't already left seemed to be posting from their social media accounts from the long queues to check-in desks and security, passports in hand.

"What is it now? I don't know how much more I can handle. Oh, we stopped to raid that plum tree, the one in Lower Valley. It was bent over double and fruit just-turn. The way we both love them. Why are you looking at me like that? I nearly broke my neck in a skirt and heels filling a plastic bag just for you."

"You ain't gon' like this." Lorna was seriously getting on her nerves with her hesitant approach to the leak or lack of storm shutters that she was about to share. "I don't like it so you ain't gon' like it."

"Lorna, please. Just spit it out."

"I went to Missy and Busta Smythe's room to get them packed up and out in a car to the airport."

"Oh good. I'm glad. Oren invited them to stay with him but I think if anything gets serious they might be better off on the mainland."

"Tha's the problem."

"You didn't get them packed and to the airport then? How are we going to manage all this and get them off to the airport as well? I hear that people are lined up around the terminal and on the tarmac."

"Dammit, Sharon. Would you just hush up and listen to me? No, I didn't."

"Shit, Lorna. Shit. As if we didn't have enough—"

"Listen. Just listen to me before you get upset. 'Cause I got plenty for you to get upset about. I went there this mornin' like we'd agreed. The card reader on the door got a piece o' tape over it and an envelope marked please read, do not open door."

"What was in the envelope?"

"Sit down." Lorna presented Sharon with a note written on creamy stationery. "Sit down. Please."

Ruby & Leland Smythe

Dear Friends,

First of all, a great big thank you is in order. Not just for this trip to the Corniche, but every stay since the very first. For as far back as we can remember, we've been coming here at least twice a year. Sometimes more often. Now that I sit here and think back, it's more like three visits per year. There has always been a nice long stay just before the kids went back to school to commemorate the end of summer vacation. They would go back physically exhausted with peeling noses but minds clear and ready for the year ahead, thanks to you. We have never forgotten that early summer when the kids got sea urchins in the bottoms of their feet and Miss Lorna ordered them out of the lobby to go pee on themselves, and each other.

Then, as the kids got older they went to boarding school and then university, and we kept coming on our own. Then they grew up, got married and started families of their own and we would often come with additional family members. We would still steal away in the late summer sometimes during that lull between seasons. But we almost never missed our annual winter visit to Cayman and the Corniche just to be able to escape the cold. But we have also come to celebrate our small and significant life events, recoup from loss and recover from illness. You know how it is. Well maybe you don't. You have endured just about as much of winter as you can and you can't stand a moment more, or endure another storm. This place has become as much a second home as it has a family tradition.

I realized some time ago that we had stopped asking for things or making special requests for anything, and that's because whatever we needed just seemed to appear. A pot of coffee in the morning, a bottle of spring water down on the beach, a pot of some exotic tea made from the steeped leaves of a local bush because Miss

Lorna knew that it would help with post-chemo nausea and fatigue or morning sickness. These things always seem to turn up in front of us a minute or two before we even think of requesting them. For this, we are so very grateful.

This place has become a second home to us. There weren't that many lodging choices in those early days. The Corniche looked remote and lonely during those early years when there was no development to the north and south. I still remember going into George Town and hearing the local community refer to it as Goldberg's Folly! Other hotels eventually sprung up, as well as villas and condos on either side of the road but back then there were no sidewalks along the beach road or other landmarks or signs to help you find your way, except for those Accident: Black Spot signs that were supposed to remind you to stick to the 40 mph speed limit. Remember when the speed limit around here was 40?!

But there has been no other place that we ever wanted to sleep while here in Cayman. You have all become our friends and we would like to explain to all of you what's happened. Especially you, Oren. We're so sorry for the inconvenience. We have enjoyed robust good health for most of our lives. For most of our marriage, Lee and I have been the picture of health. Until recently, that is. The cancer that I thought I'd beaten a few years ago is back and has metastasized to my ribs, lung and most recently my liver. The pain is becoming unbearable. Lee has been battling Parkinson's, which some of you might have begun to notice this last year or two. Now it turns out he's also in the early stages of dementia. We've thought it through and wanted to take some sort of control over what's happening to us. We also agreed that we couldn't bear the thought of one of our kids or grandchildren dropping in unannounced (they all have keys and free reign of the fridge) and our housekeeper is almost as old and frail as we are. I have taken the precaution of placing this note outside our door as well as some tape and paper over the card reader. Please take your time when calling the authorities.

Lastly, we wanted to do something beautiful. Lee's attorney has been left with instructions for the creation of a trust to finance the education of the Corniche's staff and your children. It will be there and available for as long as there is a Corniche for you and your loved ones. Please use it.

With our gratitude for all these years, your kindness and the many sunsets,

Ruby & Lee

Sharon didn't understand what was happening. She could sense Lorna's mounting frustration with her. But try as she might, her mind just wasn't allowing her to connect the dots. It was as if she was having to manually cancel the auto-pilot that had taken her through the last two weeks and line her mind up for landing the old-fashioned way.

"No," finally managed to make its way from her mouth. "No."

"Sharon, you need to try so stay calm."

"Lorna, do you understand this? Do you understand what this means?"

"I understand it fine. Do you?"

"Oh dear God. What have we done?"

"I just showed you the letter, didn't I?"

"No. I mean, what have we done? Have you gone into the room? Or called an ambulance? Your first aid training is up to date. You didn't have to wait for me. You know CP..."

"No. Sharon, listen to what you' sayin' here. This ain't no medical emergency now. This is..."

"Don't say it. Don't. I can't believe this. Have you just been sitting waiting? We have to, I mean I have to..."

"No, Sharon. You don't need to see that, I can't go in there and see that".

Sharon looked down to find that Lorna had clamped her about the wrists, drawing her close and restraining her movement. She still didn't quite understand that these guests, everybody's friends, were...were...

"We don't have a minute to lose, Lorna."

"Sharon, you ain't proposin' that we break in there and try to revive them two old people or somehow try to save the day, now? Or call for an ambulance?"

Somewhat to Lorna's surprise, Sharon stopped to ponder these questions, and their options. Sharon had so gallantly and admirably taken the reins during their most recent crisis, but she seemed to be having difficulty with this one. Lorna led the shell-shocked manager down to the beach, which was thankfully deserted as the island was preparing for Tropical Storm Lisa. The lack of people reminded Lorna of days long gone, when it was possible to walk a mile or two and never encounter another body, least of all one as scantily clad as those that usually washed up on their shores today. The Corniche's furniture had already been stored, and Lorna was forced to push Sharon down to sit on a step, where she put her face in her hands and took several purposeful breaths.

"I guess I don't agree with it. You know. Assisted suicide and abortion and stuff like that."

"I wouldn't be fond o' either decision myself."

"But you would be able to comply with their wishes? I mean they're not requesting we do anything per se, but I get what they're asking for by doing it here. Wait as long as possible before picking up the phone and dialling 999."

"All they's asking for is that we don't interfere. And wait. I will do that for them but we need to agree."

"You know, I didn't bat an eyelash last time when it came to – him. You were in shock, Oren had regressed back to childhood and I knew I had to make a decision. The right decision." Lorna was slightly surprised at Sharon's resilience and ability to recover her ability to think clearly. This sort of thinking was not typical of Sharon's pretty little head, and yet it was becoming more common in recent weeks. "And if I had to do it all over again, I would. No regrets. So I don't understand why I feel so upset and involved and complicit with what's happening to those lovely people upstairs."

"Because they was nice people. That's why. They was friends to us all and I'll miss them and I would worry about you if you didn't feel like this 'cause it would mean that you got no heart. As for having issues with what they done, if you got a problem with it then don't do what they done. That's all I can tell you."

"You seem so sure about this."

"No. They was real nice people and I wish there was more that I could do."

"Are we doing the right thing?"

"Depends on your point o' view. Second time in a month that we needed to decide what the best thing was and just go ahead and do it."

"And then there's the negative publicity to consider when this hits the Marl Road." Sharon looked up and stared at Lorna with wide eyes. "Oren! Oh my God, Lorna. What are we going to do with him? We're going to have to go tell him first and he's going to be a basket case."

"We'll do what we always do with each other on this team. We play to strengths and bolster them up when it comes to weaknesses. In his case he gon' need a diaper and a good shoulder to cry on. And we gon' sit here and get real calm and take our time before we seek him out and hopefully another hour will have passed before we find him."

"You just sit and breathe, baby. Just breathe, and when you feel better I gon' go get you something sweet to drink."

"No I'm fine, honestly. Don't leave me here by myself."

"I nuh goin' nowhere. I done told you that."

They sat looking out at the surf washing up the beach ahead of them.

***

Oren made it easy for them to decide when the right time would be to call the authorities. He had needed sedating. He was asleep in Penthouse 4 as the paramedics locked the doors of the second ambulance while Lorna and Sharon looked on from the peripherals, arm in arm.

"Oh, God," said Sharon for about the tenth time.

"At least they had each other," answered Lorna. "They was real lucky."

"You think?"

"They lived together."

"But to go like this..."

"Well, they don't know, wherever they is," answered Lorna, trying to suppress her annoyance.

"I guess you're right."

"I can't tell you how many times I've looked at them two and wished I'd either had an easier life or someone to share the difficulties of this one with. It sure ain't been easy at a table for one."

"I can imagine."

"Oh well. No time to feel sorry for muhself but when things like this happen, they make you reflect."

"Reflect? On what?"

"Everythin' and all. People doin' important jobs. Police, paramedics. They get me thinkin' y' know. I sure wish life had been one little bit easier. Even with this job. I go home, too tired most evenings to be able to do anything more than sort out tomorrow's uniform."

"What would you have done differently?"

"Law school. Chartered accounting? I don't know."

"I'm not really sure why I would have to be the one to point this out to you Lorna" Sharon hesitated

"Wha?"

"Both of these do-over situations would have you no happier than you are right now."

"Why you say that?" Lorna indignant at Sharon's dismissal of her daydream.

"Because I happen to know that you would have been the most unsuccessful quixotic bleeding heart attorney that this island would have ever seen. You'd make even less money than you do now. Fighting for every lost cause that sat down and pled its case at your desk."

"What you talkin' bout?"

"Admit it. You wouldn't be a hotshot lady lawyer, renowned for deals and takeovers and acquisitions. You would be in the family law courts day in and day out fighting for causes that just don't pay. Am I wrong?" Sharon knew that Lorna didn't like hearing this. The silence that followed meant that she was entirely right. "Lorna, what is so terribly wrong with your life?"

"Nothin', Sharon. Nothin' at all. Only that I coulda did so much more with it."

"Such as?"

"OK, maybe not a lawyer. University. Medical school. I don' know but I can tell you sometimes I wish I knew more than ground truth. Did you know that some people get paid to go into other people houses and organize they closets and clothes and stuff?" Something in Lorna stopped her from mentioning Mrs Smythe's suggestion any more explicitly.

"Lorna, you have a stable job. You're valued. You're appreciated."

"I'm housekeepin' Sharon. I am the maid."

"You can add columns of numbers in your head. You've got common sense and street smarts, and you know that it's not too late to do something else if you want to."

"I don' know which terrifies me more. The idea of the somethin' else or plannin' to stay put."

21.

"Oren? Louis, here. How are you?" Louis Bodden almost always began his phone calls like this, as if he was calling from the continent circa 1930 and they had just been connected by an operator sitting at her switchboard rather than calling a mobile which automatically displayed his name. Oren wouldn't be have been surprised if the call had begun with "Mr Goldberg? I have Mr Bodden on the line. Hold, please."

"How the hell are you?" asked Louis. "Looks as if we're in for a blowjob. Lisa is heading straight our way. Are you ready?"

"As ready as I can be." Oren wasn't in the mood for small talk. The call meant that Louis was fishing for something. But first, he would spin it to sound as though he was doing Oren the Mitzvah . Surely he must have heard the news by now. Was he going to say nothing?

"I'll get straight to the point as we're both busy. I have a consortium who have asked me to approach you and see if you might be interested in a sale."

"A sale?"

"Yes. The hotel, lock stock and barrel. I realise that you would have to approach your shareholders and reach and try to reach a consensus but considering your finances I thought that it might be something to think about."

"My finances? What about my finances?"

"Well, there has been some talk in town about a little cashflow trouble over there. You know how people like to gossip."

Oren paused before answering. A lifetime of living and working in Cayman meant that he knew how to handle gossip just as well as the yentas who often called to spread it, often passing themselves off as well-wishing do-gooders. He knew that should never get too excited because this could be construed by the other party as a confession or admission.

"Well, I wouldn't say that, Louis. It's been a slow summer, but I'm sure we'll be fine. High season is almost here." Also, never admit or deny either. It was always best to be as fake as possible; deflect then try to change the subject. It hardly mattered. Louis launched into his sales pitch, attempting to convince Oren that this was a huge favour with an approaching expiration date. "Besides. I think it's safe to say that consensus to sell is never going to happen."

Oren knew that the prospects looked rather dim, possibly approaching darkness. But he had to consider the facts. The Corniche and the land that it sat on would probably sell for enough to solve his and everyone else's problems. He knew that Bobby was still holding onto the hope that there might be some spare cash somewhere to help send him to school. However, there was probably not even enough to cover the bank fees and keep open the account that had once sent Sharon away, some years back . Having to admit to the boy that both he and the hotel were too short of cash to help with his tuition and expenses was going to be heartbreaking. They simply hadn't made enough money these past few years.

"Oren, you know that the cost of insurance goes up with every storm that visits, and here comes another one. I just thought I might advise you that this could be a good time to get a written agreement shored up. Even if you make it through this one unscathed, the price of doing business will go up yet again.

"Thank you, Louis. I appreciate your kind advice as always, but we're swamped with too many other issues right now. Maybe we can revisit this after the storm has passed."

"Oh yes. Well, you know me," Louis answered, far too smugly for Oren's liking. "Always looking for a way to lend a hand but bear in mind that if you suffered any significant damage, the offering price would go down in a matter of days. I'm here to help if you ever need me." Sure you are, thought Oren as their trunk call came to an end. Could this possibly be the universe finding a way to tell him that it was finally time? His answer? Everybody's answer? If he could sell the place for, say, fifty million or so, it would be more than enough to pay everyone, send Bobby off to school, settle up with the banks, get Lorna comfortably retired and maybe even be left with an additional five to retire with himself. Maybe he should get back to Louis and ask for this group to come up with an offer.

But on second thoughts, he decided to wait.

*

They all knew what had happened to the Smythes and the decision Ruby and Lee had made to check out. There was now a quiet, respectful resignation within the group of their friends and colleagues. A private memorial would have to be planned for a later date. The island was still preparing for the arrival of Tropical Storm Lisa, and while the topic of the double suicide was possibly being discussed in circles removed from the Corniche, those who were mourning them felt reassured that they were being allowed the dignity of getting lost in a particularly noisy news cycle.

There was a sombre sense of sadness in the Goldberg house that morning, and it merged with the unspoken fear of the approaching storm to create a mood that no one there could find an adjective for. The tragedy was not discussed there, not least of all because of the possibility that overhearing it would deepen Oren's sadness. Sharon had decided to remind the staff not to discuss the situation in public, whether verbally, by email: but a memo to this effect pinned to the back office notice board was not only unnecessary but would have seemed insensitive if not insulting. She hadn't needed to. In the 48 hours between the coroner's arrival and their reunion at Oren's, the tragedy had barely even been broached among them, and Sharon found herself having to break the unspoken rule to enquire about Oren.

"Is Oren alright?" she asked in a loud whisper before even saying hello upon arrival.

"As right as you can expect. They was like a aunt and uncle to him."

"Funny. That's sort of how I think of them. A benevolent old aunt and uncle."

"I reckon that's how we all gon' think of them," answered Lorna as she stoically reflected on her memories of the kind old pair that she had come to love. By now, everyone who needed to know or whose children might one day benefit from Ruby and Lee's bequest had been apprised of their gift. Bobby seemed to assume that this meant his tuition would be taken care of, and for now no one was telling him otherwise.

"That reminds me, Lorna. Have you given any more thought to your own career?"

"Me?! Nah. Too late now for me."

"To upgrade your skills? Even a dangerous chemicals course? Or a first aid refresher? Or something more ambitious?"

"Too late to do anything like that now," answered Lorna who assumed that Sharon couldn't sense the anxiety that this suggestion was releasing.

"It's never too late, Lorna." Sharon did know that Lorna held some deep-seated emotion, a kind of frustration or inadequacy. But the nature of this feeling was just out of her emotional grasp. "If you were to call about late registration, I bet you'd be surprised to see how many mature students you would find at your first lecture."

"Lecture?" asked Lorna incredulously. "Me? You have got to be jokin' Sharon."

"No. All you have to do is..."

"Sharon you know damn well that I never seen the inside of a lecture hall and the only way I can go to university now is if we go belly-up and I end up cleanin' one."

"Why the hell not? Your accounting skills are a whole lot better than mine. Or do something totally unrelated just for fun."

"I can hear the talk in George Town now. Look at that fool Lorna Ebanks sittin' up in there, like she can learn. Boy, she must think high of herself. Like she smart or somethin'."

"But you are smart, Lorna. You're just scared, that's all." Sharon said in a reassuring voice. Lorna wanted to keep discussing this about as much as she wanted to admit the crippling fear that had come over her just from imagining herself in a room full of students with some sort of lecturer in front, looking back at her. Staring down at her.

"Honestly, Lorna. Why are you getting so testy with me? Fine. If you don't want to go, then don't. Stay home. Watch reruns of the same old shows until you run out of episodes for all I care. But you're barely fifteen years older than me. What huge difference could there be between us that makes an evening course so foreign to you?"

"Confidence," answered her cousin, flatly. "Confidence and a lack of regret and not givin' a damn when you walk into a room with people in it and all the heads look your way."

"Oh, honey. We all have something or other that gives us butterflies." But again, Sharon's attempt to comfort her cousin had precisely the opposite effect – Lorna just threw her hands in the air and returned to the kitchen.

***

"Is this what it's like? We basically just sit here and wait for Hurricane Lisa to arrive?"

"What else you want us to do? Call feh expedited delivery?"

"Yeah. Sorry. Silly question. I guess there's not much we can do. It's just...it's just that I've never had to sit and wait for a hurricane before."

They were in the lovely drawing room of the Goldberg residence. The questions were being asked by Lolly, the new girl. Her presence was good news to Lorna. It meant that anyone else arriving could speculate about her, and not about the romance between Sharon and Hugh that had come out of the closet with their arrival together and use of the same guest room.

"Tha's okay. Jus' don't use the 'H' word. She's still a tropical storm. Don't call it down."

"Sorry."

Miss Lorna nodded her absolution. "Don' worry, baby. We knows this your first time. Imagine how they mussah felt in thirty-two with only a barometer. At least we got some fair warnin'."

"What's it like, then? The noise? The thunder and lightning?"

Lorna sat down on the tufted pouffe that she knew was supposed to be called an ottoman at Oren's but she still called a pouffe, partly to get on his nerves and partly because she didn't think it was nice to sit on something named after other people's countries. "Some say the noise is only so loud as the silence that leads up to it. But hurricanes don't bring that much thunder or lightnin' once they on top o' you. That's something that'll surprise you, no doubt. It's the wind and the rain and the sound of impact."

"Impact?" Lolly's eyes widened. The wind was barely starting yet and Lorna could see that this girl was going to take a lot of maintenance. Or liquor. Or sedating.

"Hurricane can lift and blow a small car across yuh line o' sight and the sea can take tons o' sand an' pile it up in front o' you while you watchin'. You'd be surprised at the sound objects make when they meet mid-air. Even rain bein' hurled horizontally at a hundred miles an hour has its own sound. That alone is a noise that could set you crazy."

"But we're prepared, right?'

Lorna nodded. "Now if y'all will excuse me, I'm goin' to the kitchen to start bakin' chickens." She got up and left. She liked to stay busy when times got tough. Oren was playing the host, although each time she saw him from the corner of her eye he was wearing another piece of chef's attire. She expected to see those expensive-looking suede loafers ruined in the kitchen. If she was cooking she'd be damned if she was going to clean as well; she couldn't wait to see him with a mop.

There was a shallow, covered container on the bottom shelf of the oven, cooking ever so slowly. She had managed to convince Clive, her third cousin and local farmer, that it was better to slaughter a cow this week and sell her the best cuts at cost than to risk the cow being blown off the face of the earth. She had also ordered six baking chickens from Kingston via the Corniche's supplier. They tasted better than their American cousins – rusty, salty and like the chickens of her childhood that had been slaughtered, prepared and eaten the same day. She was about to tackle the first three when the swinging door into the kitchen opened and Sir Hugh walked in. To Lorna's great surprise, he offered his assistance as a sous-chef.

"You knows how tuh cook?" She folded her arms and eyed him up and down.

"Try me," he answered. "My spine may be turning to powder, but as long as I can sit or lean and the work is in front of me, you might be surprised at what I can accomplish. Besides, I want to see your secrets. Especially the beef."

"It's called Cayman beef for a reason. The recipe is in my head and it ain't leavin' this island. But since you here," she said as she brought over a knife, chopping board and a sack of shallots, "start choppin'. Soon-come. I left my apron in muh overnight bag."

Oren seemed to be waiting for her at the bottom of the stairs. With no drink in his hand, his body language seemed awkward and agitated to her. He looked irritable and although she loved the man far more when he was slightly liquored up, Lorna suspected that she well knew what was wrong with him. His plans to hold court for the duration of the storm were not going as planned.

She could see it now. Sir Hugh wasn't in the library of the Goldberg house, sitting in one of those ridiculous wingback- knockoff chairs sipping cognac from an oversized snifter. In Oren's fantasy, Sharon's man would probably be wearing a smoking jacket, monogrammed velvet slippers and discussing the most recent episode of *Masterpiece Theatre* with Oren, who would be in the companion chair swirling his own golden liquid in a glass.

"Everything okay?" he asked as he watched her put on her tattered apron.

"Ship-shape. You lookin' somethin' to do? Come peel these potatoes feh mih." She had a feeling that he wasn't going to appreciate the dynamic in the kitchen and she was looking forward to that. He followed her, not quite knowing what to do with himself despite having a houseful of people to entertain.

"I didn't know that you have to use coconut milk and an entire branch of thyme in a pot of rice and peas," Sir Hugh was saying as Oren followed Lorna into the kitchen that he used so rarely. Hugh appeared to be following Lorna's requests to the letter dicing several pounds of shallots. Now he was now slicing pieces of raw coconut into a slowly purring Cuisinart. Oren placed himself where he could stand behind Lorna's shoulder and watch her pressing the pureed coconut meat through a Chinese hat strainer into the large copper pot of long grain rice. It looked like another PBS series altogether, one of those later Julia Child programmes in which she loomed over the guest chef who was demonstrating a technique while Julia waited patiently to sample whatever it was that was being prepared.

"Yah, man. Now I like to squeeze all the liquid outta the pulp before dumping it too," said Lorna as she demonstrated this, before placing several large stalks of thyme on top of the rice and putting it over a low flame. Lorna knew that Oren had been reading his Burke's Peerage before people had started arriving to his not-so-little hurricane party; soon he would be telling her how many rules of British etiquette she was breaking by agreeing to Sir Hugh's request to teach him a few Caymanian recipes to take back to London. Hearing her address Sir Hugh casually would be having an effect on Oren, and the fleeting look of annoyance on his face gave her a little frisson of satisfaction. "Now," she asked Sir Hugh while dusting off her hands, "which other trade secret you wan' take home with you?"

"I want to know what went into the stuffing for those chickens, and the rum punch and the swanky."

"You want to know what goes in my swanky? You mussah jokin." Lorna threw her head back and laughed.

Oren backed out of the kitchen, retreating to search for Sharon. He didn't quite know why he didn't want this sort of thing going on, but he was feeling uncomfortable. Sharon was tucked away in a corner, trying to read a novel on a window seat, biting her lip and wrinkling her brow as she looked out at the worsening weather.

"Have you seen Sir Hugh and Lorna?" Oren asked.

"Last I checked they were swapping state secrets in the kitchen. She was teaching him rice and peas and when I left, she was sweet-talking him into stuffing orange slices and garlic cloves up the rear ends of chickens. They're fine. Why do you ask?"

"Well, it's just that I wondered if it was okay with you for Lorna to flirt with your boyfriend like that."

Sharon didn't bother to look up. "Fine by me. She needs the practice, and he needs to learn how to use salt and pepper,"

He sat down at the window seat, his hands in his lap. "What's the matter? Tell me," demanded Sharon, putting the book down.

"You know how it gets in a storm. Even if we try to stay out of each other's hair over the next day or two, we'll have gotten on each other's last nerve by the time it's over. Lorna tends to take over. And she doesn't know how to speak to the landed gentry."

"He's not landed gentry. Here he's just Hugh. Let him stick his hand up a chicken's ass and let her boss him around a kitchen. It'll do them both good."

"She does it at the hotel too. Dahlin' and Chile and Baby."

"It's why they all loves her so. And don't forget we have politicians in the House who used the same terms of endearment on everybody from Kate Middleton to Baroness Scotland. Maybe even the Queen. Chill a bit. Relax. We're all fine. Feel like getting your ass whipped at dominoes?"

"Try me."

"Let's go check on everyone and make sure their drinks are filled. The hotelier in me can't help it."

"Neither can the drinker," replied Sharon as she opened a Red Stripe, hoping to save herself a trip back to the kitchen.

Miss Lorna was back in the sitting room, trying to talk Lolly down while Bobby stroked her shoulder. Someone always cracked first, she thought to herself. It was beginning.

"Chile, they call it the calm before the storm for good reason. Now you sit through that calm and wait. We all sit here and wait and wonder and worry and ask if it was necessary to go through all this trouble."

Lorna knew that sitting and waiting for a storm to arrive could be difficult for a young person who had never experienced it, and she tried her very best to remain calm and help Lolly. She knew that waiting often made it feel as though time had slowed down. In her own case, it was vital that she stay busy or she would end up in front of one of the house's windproof windows wringing her hands and worrying about her garden.

"That was a rare display of patience, Lorna," said Oren as he entered the kitchen to continue overseeing her work.

"I can be patient. I just choose not to most days. It takes too much outta you."

"Too much patience," he added, thinking himself witty.

Lorna turned to return to the kitchen. She couldn't stand another moment of tedium. What if she ran out of things to do, and animal carcasses to stuff? She was considering graduating from her second Red Stripe to something stronger when the doorbell rang.

"Oren," she bellowed. Who else you gon' invite to this party? I sure hope they brought ice." No one appeared to be getting up to answer; Lorna made her way to the large, weatherproof double doors, beer still in hand, to let in the last of the guests. Just a few years ago, Lorna might well have flung the door open without asking who was on the other side, and peepholes were a recent detail in new homes, but something told her to look out before welcoming the latest arrival.

"Suh hep muh Crise. Oren. You best get out here an' bring Sharon with you," she bellowed into the bowels of the house and composing herself before opening the door.

"I do hope that I'm not imposing, Miss Lorna," said a perfectly turned out Ms Davis, waiting on the step. "It's just that I was hoping to have a quick word with Mr Goldberg if it's not inconvenient. I was hoping to get out on the last flight and I've got just enough time to chat and make my way back to the airport."

"Not at all, Doooo come in," replied Lorna in her best attempt at sounding stush. She knew that there was something grave about to be revealed. She could just feel it Oren had moved on to making a mess in the kitchen, attempting simultaneous preparation of unidentified courses of a yet-to-be-determined meal. He had still to supply his guests with so much as a quail's egg on a cracker, but came out of the kitchen's swinging door wearing a chef's hat and an apron with an obscene message printed on the front. Like a toddler, thought Lorna. Turn your back on him for a moment...

"Hello, Mrs ...ummh...Miss..."

"Ms Davis," said Bobby, coming into the foyer.

"Hello Bobby," said Ms Davis, offering the boy a smile.

"Oh yes. Of course. Do come in Ms Davis. Can I get you a sherry?" Oren asked as he ushered her into his study.

"Or I can fix you a cocktail?" asked Bobby. "I've got everything prepared and the glasses are chilled and you wouldn't even know we weren't by the pool."

"No. No, thank you. I won't be long. I just need a quiet word with Mr Goldberg."

Sharon took this to mean that she wouldn't be needed, but Lorna grabbed her by the arm and beckoned for her to wait outside the study doors.

"He can't deal with her without help," she said as she let go of Sharon's arm.

"A sherry? Now I ask you. What the hell Oren think this is? Downton fuckin' Abbey?" Lorna asked Bobby, who was standing there confused and waiting for instructions.

"I'll wait right here, Miss Lorna," said the bartender. "In case a champagne cocktail will help. I wonder what that's all about?"

"I guess we's about to find out," answered Lorna as she and Sharon continued to listen at the door.

It was less than a minute later when they were beckoned into the study by the sound of Oren desperately bellowing their names. But it was slightly more than a summoning. Oren sounded as though he was about to drown and was calling for them to jump into the deep end of the pool after him.

"I wish you weren't right so often," said Sharon.

Goldberg and Davis were at opposite ends of the little room. Oren was obviously retreating as far away from the guest as he could possibly get. He pointed to a shiny little object in Ms Davis' hand, which she was holding out triumphantly.

"As I was just saying to Mr Goldberg, you would never believe what I found along the cliffs of Pedro St. James the other night while I was out for a moonlit stroll." Lorna and Sharon crept closer to look into the lady's hand. Staring up at them was Sharon's name tag.

"Oh Christ. Christ alla-mighty."

"Now then. It would appear to me that you have something that belongs to me and vice versa. And we're not talking about Paul's body. I would appreciate having the contents of his hotel room. You know what I mean."

22.

"Northwest Caribbean Prepares for Direct Hit as Lisa Approaches"

Bobby's crush on Ms Davis was well documented and discussed in the back rooms of the Corniche. "Your girlfriend's waiting for you at the bar," was all he needed to hear to motivate him to cut his breaks short and return to his post. It was sitting here in the library of the Goldberg house that he realized that he had been a silly boy. She was quickly falling from her pedestal and he observed her halo beginning to tarnish. She wasn't nearly as lovely as she once seemed. It seemed like a short eternity before anything happened. He couldn't help but wonder if someone hadn't flipped a switch responsible for stopping the passage of time and was not happy to hear that Oren's was the first mouth to open.

"Oh my God, Lorna. She found it on the ironshore behind Pedro Castle!"

"Oren, would you hush up?" she snapped. Bobby wasn't sure what was happening as he watched Mr Goldberg self-consciously pop his mouth shut as Miss Lorna returned her attention to the uppity white woman, as she always referred to Ms Davis, and who she had been longing to punch out for some time.

"So? That don't mean nothin," she answered with her dominoes face.

"Oh, but I'm afraid it does, Miss Lorna," said Miss Davis smugly.

"Only that Sharon likes to take walks along the ironshore down by Pedro St. James to get a breath o' fresh air or clear her head. Unless you got somethin' to say to me, I got people to cook for and you needs to get to a shelter 'cause we's all full up here." This wasn't exactly true. Nothing needed tending to and there was more than enough room for more guests. But if this woman stayed around much longer, Lorna was going to have to resist the urge to beat her to the floor with that big orange Birkin bag she was lugging around, or strangle her with one of its lovely straps. "This ain't the Corniche and I be damned if I got to sit here and listen to you poppy-show of a white waif talk down to me."

"Well that would depend on the reason for the walk, I suppose. And the company. Oh, and the cargo in the back of Mr Goldberg's car, wrapped up in a lovely tapis from the Corniche. Funny to be disposing of them like that. They look rather expensive."

"We got no comment," answered Miss Lorna, holding her palm out to Oren who seemed about to explode, or vibrate or emote himself to death. But she would be damned if she would let him crumble or even so much as speak.

"Are you sure? I mean, are you quite sure? Would you still not like to say something? Even if I was to tell you that I had timestamped photos of the three of you? Miss Lorna, Miss Phelan and you, Mr Goldberg. And it was far more than a walking meeting. Far more than a search for fresh air. You appeared to be disposing of what appeared to be a human body."

"What were you doing there?" asked Oren, causing Lorna even more visible agitation.

"Following you."

"Look lady. I ain't got no idea what you getting' at but I got three people's work to do, I ain't gettin' paid for it and if you was expectin' an invitation to stay, then you'd best be on your way to the nearest hurricane shelter because I ain't buyin' what you sellin' in that expensive handbag. Just give us the Watchtower and Bible and message from Jesus and get on."

"That really is a lovely Birkin bag." Mr Goldberg, looking as though hoping to disarm the tension regarded what was clearly an expensive handbag that sat next to the uninvited guest. It had the opposite effect. Ms Davis nodded her approval. Lorna's reaction was exasperated.

Except for Lolly who had disappeared upstairs to her room, they were now all in the library, surrounding the uninvited guest. Bobby still had no idea what they were talking about, but it looked serious. And the weather seemed to be getting worse every time he looked through what he knew were expensive panes of glass. It was the first time Bobby had ever stared at anything other than a storm shutter or a piece of nailed plywood in a storm event and he didn't know if he preferred it. Maybe it was better not to have windows during a storm. You had to force yourself to take your eyes away; plus the tension in the room was making him feel uneasy.

"Well isn't this cosy? I love a house with a library." Ms Davis seemed to think that she was chairing the meeting.

"Yes, ma'am. Real civilized." Miss Lorna had no intention of letting up any control. She stood there, staring down the other woman, her arms folded in that way that was strictly against the rules anywhere at the Corniche.

"And I believe that we are all caught up in the same intrigue."

"What she talkin' 'bout?" asked Lorna, to no one in particular, attempting to bluff.

"Maybe we should all just try to relax and have a cool drink and a nice pleasant chat," said Mr Goldberg diplomatically. Unsurprisingly no one acknowledged this.

"Look, I'll get to the point. I don't want to be stuck on your lovely little island during a storm, but I felt as though I had to come in person and request the return of something that belongs to me. And I'm not referring to the body. Thank you, by the way."

"For whah'?"

"For getting rid of him. I don't know what inspired you or how you did it, but I do appreciate it." Miss Lorna seemed to swell. From her sharp intake of breath it was clear this was not going to end well.

"What inspired it? What inspired it? The man attacked me."

"I regret that. I do. You see, I had hoped that he would save me the trouble of having to put a bullet through him. So messy. Instead, I fed him a rather healthy dose of LSD in a glass of champagne and suggested he jump off the balcony or anything else that would look like a suicide. Then I went down to the bar and got a good seat to wait for the show. Unfortunately, you went in to clean about an hour later and I was left with only Bobby for entertainment."

Bobby, who remained silent until he heard his name, now made his presence known.

"Wait, what? You mean you're a...a..."

"A ginnal. A no-good con-artist. Just like her boyfriend."

"Please," interjected Miss Davis. "Paul was my mule, not my boyfriend. Which is why I'm here. I would be grateful if you three fixers could return my consignment and my pocket money."

"I don't believe it. I thought you were so classy. I thought you were like, a society lady or a banker's wife. I mean I knew you weren't famous. I couldn't find you online so I assumed you were high society."

"She a high-class somethin'. You got that part right."

"I'm running out of patience, Miss Lorna. I want my cash and my consignment."

"I hid the stash."

"Where, please?"

"Down the toilet."

"I don't understand what's happening," said Sir Hugh, who was sitting further down the table.

"Your friends appear to have killed Paul Pratt and disposed of the body."

"What?" Hugh's eyes were wide. He's dead? That horrid man? Good. Good riddance." he added, now alert and animated. "If one of you did kill him, I'll pay for your defence if you're caught. But I doubt Sharon had anything to do with it. She couldn't step on a roach."

"Or so you think, Sir Hugh. What if I was to suggest to you that your lovely Sharon was complicit in this and that this name tag is proof? Would you care to make out those cheques to me from now on? While you're in a generous mood?"

"That is highly unlikely, young lady."

"Which brings me back to the topic of the cash in Paul's room."

"There's a funny story about that," Sharon said.

"Go ahead."

"I logged it as a particularly generous gratuity and deposited into the bank."

"That's easily solved then. Un-deposit it."

"Then I wired it."

"This is getting tedious. To where, please?"

"I paid Bobby's tuition to hotel school."

"I thought you said that the hotel's scholarship fund might be able to pay for that," said Bobby, on the brink of informational overload.

"It did. With a generous gratuity, made by Ms Davis here."

"Is that how the money materialised?"

"Well it wasn't from sales," explained Lorna. "Or tips."

"Enough!" The bag was obviously expensive. Sharon found its presence on its owner's arm distracting. Now Davis reached into it and pulled out the tiniest revolver that any of them had ever seen.

"So now you're going to shoot us," Sharon said this as if it was a declaration and not a question.

"Do you people understand what I'm saying here?"

"What I'm saying is I don't give a rat's ass." So calm? Bobby had never seen a gun in his life. It wasn't a pleasant feeling, but Miss Lorna didn't flinch. How could she be so calm?

"May I remind you, Miss Lorna, that I am the one holding the gun?"

"What you got ma'am is a purse pistol with one bullet. Maybe two."

If there was one person at the Corniche that Bobby truly adored, it was Miss Lorna. Her no-nonsense delivery of common-sense ideas and lack of sentimentality were always a welcome part of his day: they regularly met in the public areas to bolster one another or commiserate in the parking lot to share the day's gossip over a cigarette. Today he noticed for the first time the vast reserves of courage that she concealed. She was confronting Ms Davis as if she, and not the other woman was holding the gun. In fact, it didn't seem as though Miss Lorna was even affected by the presence of the pistol and the barrel that was pointed in her face as she spoke. As Mr Goldberg stood by helplessly, it was Miss Lorna who was stepping up to confront the career criminal. Bobby watched in admiration as Miss Lorna continued to stare down the gun and its owner.

"Two casualties then."

"You need to go back and do the math." It was Sharon who spoke this time, surprising everyone, it seemed. "You're attempting to intimidate a room full of people but you don't have enough bullets. Even if you were to incapacitate one of us, you wouldn't make it out of this house."

"How's that?"

"Because unless you kill me first I gon' kill you with my bare hands. Look at you, woman. You think you can fight with that manicure?" said Miss Lorna.

"And if you hurt Lorna first, I will climb across this table and bitch-slap your ass into next fall's ready-to-wear collection. Don't underestimate me. I'd kill you and bury you next to the lime tree for that purse."

"Besides. We know you won't. We have the resources to put you out of business, you know. Each person in this room is either a cousin, nephew or niece to someone who could put your local business to an end, and you behind bars."

"You? The hotel staff?"

"Fact. The premier is my uncle. Lorna and I are both related to the chief of police, the chief immigration officer, the minister of finance. Shall I go on?" It was finally beginning to become apparent that Sharon and Lorna were closely related

"Do."

"If you think I won't pick up the phone and start inviting all of them to my parents for a nice turtle dinner on Friday with cornbread gossip, think again."

"You overestimate yourself."

"Have you ever heard of the Marl Road?"

"The what?"

"Marl Road. It's our equivalent of the grapevine. But it's far more useful. Or damaging in your case. And it works remarkably fast. You wouldn't want to be on the subject of some well-placed gossip."

"You're threatening to ruin my reputation? That's it? That's the best you can do?"

"Let's say you were seen at the Corniche bar with someone who resembles one of our civil servant relatives. Do you know how fast you would be declared persona non grata? We may be primitive islanders, but we have our ways of dealing with things and I think you'd be shocked at how effective our methods are."

"I'm losing my patience. And fast. I want some answers or I might have to try out this little toy after all. And it might not be here and now. It could be when you least expect it."

"Ask away."

"I want my money back[. And I want payment for that stash. My goods"

"Nothin' good about that shit."

"Don't underestimate me."

"You mean like you done to us? We might not get along. We might not like each other some days, but you threaten one o' us and you threaten us all."

"I must say. This is all very interesting. Like a quaint little conspiracy."

"No ma'am. No conspiracy. Community. No. More than that, I dare-say. Family. This here is my workplace family. We may not all be related by blood but Oren and me, we put the best years of our lives in the Corniche and I expect Sharon will be doing the same. You look at us and this place and you look down on us. Like the book done say, an island that time forgot. But while nobody was payin' attention all those hundreds o' years we learned and leaned on each other and built a barren little rock into what you see today. I think you's done here."

No one in the room ever expected the gun to go off. Least of all the person wielding it. The wind had died down again and there were a few minutes of intermittent dead silence outside, so when it suddenly and unexpectedly picked up and slammed a large piece of wooden debris against the side of the house and one of the stormproof windows, they all jumped. And Ms Davis inadvertently pulled the trigger.

The bang was deafening. Everyone seemed to jump even higher from the fright of the object on the side of the house. Sharon let out a yelp as the bullet flew sped across the room and embedded itself somewhere in the bookshelf of hardcover books that no one seemed to ever read.

"I don't believe it," said Oren after he had patted himself down to search for holes and Bobby had found the book that had been hit. "I don't fucking believe it. That was a first edition."

"I didn't mean to shoot your book," said Ms Davis, who seemed about as shocked as the others. "I only brought it for my own safety. And maybe to get my point across."

"Which means you're no longer armed," said Sharon as she and Lorna again folded their arms in unison.

"Ok look yah, Madam Davis, you just done crossed the line."

"What? Y'know, you're beginning to annoy me, chambermaid."

"An' you real facety."

"I'm not altogether sure why, but I only really understand every other word you say."

Miss Lorna set her jaw in the way she did when you knew that there was no chance of winning the argument that you might have picked but were about to lose. She pointed her chin towards her left shoulder, placing her right fist just below her waist at the right hip

"Uh-oh," said Bobby. Sharon agreed and nodded at Bobby. This woman was toast.

"I know what you see when you look around here. You see the maid, the night manager, and the boy who makes you cocktails..."

"Look, I'm in a hurry and I've read this book before – now we're probably waiting for the movie to come out. The problem is I'm out of patience. Am I going to get my money? Compensation for my goods?"

"Not any time soon. We put both to good use."

"Oh? I thought you said you flushed the drugs?"

"Well y'know, I used all that white washing powder to clean the toilet, and the mess your little friend left behind." Miss Davis's mouth opened but no sound escaped.

"Then? Then me and Oren counted all them bills and Sharon deposited it at the bank. Then that amount got wired to, how do you say it Sharon? Your alma mater? Someone will benefit from all your bullshit and schemes and deals, lady."

"Well said, Miss Lorna," said Sharon, addressing her cousin with the appropriate prefix, just for show. "And I think that I would prefer not to see you on the hotel premises again Ms Davis. If the financial situation changes anytime soon or the septic system coughs up your drugs I'll be in touch."

Bobby hadn't truly understood until now that there was a closeness between them that he hadn't been never aware of. They barely needed to talk, to communicate. It wasn't that he had underestimated Sharon, just that she always seemed to be present to take the bows on behalf of the Corniche and its staff when the hard work had been done by the rest of them. Today she was different. He had half expected her to hide when the gun came out, but she and Miss Lorna had just reached for each other's hand, each showing that they were being protective of the other. It was almost as if they had shaken hands in a silent agreement to save them all.

"I find all of this oddly heartwarming, I must say. And everyone I meet here in Cayman constantly complains of how hard it is to get good help. I can't decide whether you are fortunate, Mr Goldberg or very...yes. Yes, I think that you are a very lucky man. You have inherited a lovely hotel and surround yourself with people who care for you. You are no great hotelier, no great vision, Mr Goldberg. Cesar Ritz, you are not. I'll leave you all now to continue with your little hurricane party. But you know what?"

"What?"

"Let me tell you something – this is all far from over. You can count on me. I'll be back."

"Yes, ma'am. Very good ma'am. We'll be speaking again soon."

"Ms Davis you can't be planning to try to make your way back to town. Not now, not in this weather. Perhaps you should stay here a while."

"I appreciate the offer of hospitality but I don't see the point of sitting here and waiting for this storm to come and go."

"It probably would be safer for you to wait here."

"That sounds like an awful lot of fun but I intend to be on the next flight out. I will be fine, thank you for your concern." Lorna went to the double doors, opened one and did a rather calculated curtsey that seemed subservient, yet condescending to everyone else there. They all watched her get into her little rental car and drive through the gates heading back to town at breakneck speed.

Oren was the first to make a sound after the front door closed. He exhaled such a big breath that it seemed as though he had been holding it since Ms Davis' arrival.

"I don't believe it," he began. "That was…"

"The biggest bluff of our careers," said Sharon.

"Straight out o' the movies," declared Lorna.

"The most impressive confrontation I've ever witnessed," added Oren.

"Sharon." Hugh called Sharon's name weakly as if just sitting through the meeting was enough to exhaust him. "Sharon, do I need to hire a lawyer? I'm hardly going to miss Pratt, but is this possible? Did you kill a man?"

"Of course I didn't kill him."

"No, baby. I killed him," Miss Lorna interjected, holding up her hand as if giving an oath.

"I don't know what to believe any more." Hugh wiped his tired eyes.

"It was self-defense, Hugh. He would have raped Lorna. Or worse."

"True to Crise. If I hadn't hit him over the head I might not be here now."

"So let me get this straight. You killed Pratt, dumped the body and laundered the money in his room?"

"Yeah. I guess we did launder it. For a sound cause."

"We took dirty money and put it to good use. You goin' to university, Bobby."

"We also burned all the other trash in his room at the bottom of Oren's back yard."

"I hope you stood downwind."

23.

***** Perfect place for a staycation, bubbles, nibbles and giggles. Which is just what we plan to do as soon as you're open. —SWatler, Savannah, Newlands

"Oren? Y'alright?"

Oren sat down wearily and rubbed his eyes. Lorna could always tell when he was in one of his moods. He would need a little extra coddling today, maybe even extra dessert.

"No. I just had the craziest idea. It seemed to drop right into my head."

"Wha' happen now?"

"What if, when we get out of here and drive over to assess the damage, we find the Corniche gone? Like, obliterated off the landscape? Or sunk to the bottom of the sea? It's happened before. I remember from history class. What if we get there and the same thing happened that happened at Port Royal?"

"I don't think you need to worry about that," answered Sharon in a singsong voice that she usually reserved for unhappy guests or children in tantrums (and the occasional adult).

"What makes you so sure? So confident that it didn't happen in the night?"

"Because it was an earthquake that sank Port Royal. Are you listening? An earthquake, not a hurricane."

"Oh, yeah." Oren seemed dazed. "Sorry. I don't know what I'm talking about. I don't know what the hell's wrong with me. Well, actually maybe I do."

"You've just been through a terrible time, capped with a terrible shock and loss. I would be surprised if you weren't showing signs of the stress. They were your parents' friends. They were our friends."

"Yeah. It's not just that, though. Although I must say, Ruby and Lee do feel like the straw to my camel's back. And maybe the Corniche disappearing under the sea was more a fantasy than a fear. Part of me wouldn't be at all sorry if we got there and the whole damned place was washed out to sea somewhere. After all, the insurance is all paid up. Barely."

No one around the table was surprised to see Oren subdued, but now he sat hunched over and looking far worse than just sad, stressed and deprived of sleep.

"It's alright, baby. We know. You just talkin' like we feel." Even Lorna didn't seem to be able to get through to him this morning and he barely seemed to have noticed her attempt to comfort him.

"There's something that I feel I should tell you all." Oren sat up, straightened his back and attempted to gather himself emotionally.

"Well? Spit it out." Lorna hated it when Oren did this. She could swear that he paused like this for dramatic effect and it exasperated her no end. It often happened when he was telling a tall tale about the fish that had got away or his winnings at the casinos.

"I've been talking to someone. An old friend. He's been giving me some business advice. The guy is pretty successful, you see? And he has these clients. Some sort of consortium and they're looking for property to invest in. Anyway, they asked him to approach me about selling out."

"Well, that's exactly what it would be, Oren. Sellin' out," said Lorna without a second passing. "A sellout."

"Sell?" asked Sharon, alert and wide-eyed. "So they can knock it down and build a...a...monstrosity? After all these years? After all we've done to keep going?"

"It's not a huge parcel at the end of the day. They couldn't build anything as huge as a resort on the site. And it would be enough to retire. And I'd retire you too of course, Lorna."

"Yes, they could. They could and they would. Have you seen what they're building? Ten stories on a lot the size of a postage stamp. You'd better believe they'd knock it down." Sharon was getting mad, and Lorna would have been mildly amused at the rare sight were she not so shocked by Oren's admission.

"Oren, you mean to tell me you would actually entertain them people?"

"Yes. Not only that. After all that's happened lately I'll more than entertain them. I honestly want to call up my contact and ask him to broker an offer. I'm sorry, but I just can't take it anymore. I always thought I'd enjoy it, but the place has aged me a decade, cost me my hair and eaten up most of my capital. It's time. I've had just about enough."

Bobby watched as Lorna and Sharon once again stood, approached Oren and stopped barely a foot away from him. Sharon put an arm around Lorna, who was now getting visibly upset. For the second time since he had been barricaded in this house, he watched them stand together and pool their strength.

"Well you can't. You hear me? I cleaned plenty more toilets in that place than you, so don' tell me you had enough. Enough o' what?"

"Lorna's right," added Sharon as she squeezed Lorna to comfort her. "You can't sell."

"Give me a good reason why not."

"You mummeh would be broken-hearted. That's a start." Lorna was by now visibly upset. "And I don' need to tell you what yuh father would say if he could hear this."

"There's also your shareholders. I just happen to know that your shareholders will never consent to this," added Sharon.

"Who are the other shareholders?" asked Hugh timidly: he had been remaining diplomatic and silent through most of the hurricane party's outbursts, only interrupting when it seemed necessary.

"His Aunt Phyllis and Uncle Morton in New York," answered Lorna over her shoulder.

"And Lorna and me," added Sharon defiantly. Hugh sat up.

"You, Sharon? You never told me that you own an interest in the Corniche."

"It's pretty recent. Oren cut me a share certificate after the Pratt incident."

"I did it for some peace and quiet," answered Oren. "Another terrible deal. I'm just not good at business."

"I was already heavily invested in the place when you wrote me into the books, but I appreciate the gesture. Now the only one who isn't invested is you, Bobby. And I think that Mr Goldberg should extend the same gesture to you. Don't you think?"

"I appreciate it, Sharon. But I couldn't ask for that. Remember, I'm about to go to hotel school on a fully paid scholarship."

"What about me?" asked Hugh. "I have no interest in the Corniche."

"Let me guess? You want shares in this money pit too? Why not? How many do you want?

"Yes, yes I think that maybe I would. But perhaps more than one or two. And in my case, I'm willing to pay for them. Could we discuss it before you reach out to your contacts, Mr Goldberg?"

"I'd be happy to, Sir Hugh. Remind me again, please. What sort of business is it that you're in again?"

"Real estate, mostly. And Infrastructure. Some green energy and my company owns interest in an airline. But no hotels yet. I would like to expand into hospitality if the right project came along. Especially if I could find one with a sound management team that requires little or no management or attention from me. What do you think?"

The sound of an opening door caught all of them off guard.

"Did I miss anything?" asked Lolly, rubbing her eyes. "I fell asleep with my headphones on during my David Icke podcast."

"No, baby. You didn't miss nothing at all."

"It's almost recreational, isn't it? Like a weekend in the country."

"Yeah, on the surface, I suppose that's how it might look," said Sharon, trying to shift gears and improvise a response.

"But it's not? Come on. We've been here for a day, playing crossword puzzles, cards and dominoes. We've been through a case of wine and Red Stripe."

"It helps, you know. We all have memories of a shared history. Collective pain. The mention of a storm is enough to send anyone here into a panic."

"Funny. This feels more like a party than a hurricane."

"Think of it more like a wake that we get together to reenact every decade or so. And please stop invoking the H-word."

"What now?"

Now we wait. We've got anywhere from twelve to thirty hours to get by without getting on one another's nerves. Eat, drink and be mindful."

Bobby gazed again beyond the hurricane-proof glass of the picture window towards the west and the more populated coast of Grand Cayman: "You sure we'll be okay here, Miss Lorna? It feels like the ass-end of nowhere out here."

"We gon' be fine here baby how your mama? You sure she wouldn't be safer here with us? If we were to get a direct hit, this is still the safest place I know."

"My mother is fine, thanks for asking. She's happy and comfortable in a hotel somewhere in Miami. If I know her, she's picked up her car, dropped off her bags and is burning off the calories walking around the mall as we speak."

"As long as she's okay."

*

Allen and Gilbert had blown the grass off her front lawn, and Lorna preferred to not even think about Ivan. But she certainly knew how to prepare a household and family for a hurricane. She had enough corned beef and boxed milk stored in her own home to survive the end of the world. By midnight all the radio stations were going off the air, save the one emergency service, and it was from this tired broadcaster, struggling to stay awake in her bunker that houseguests kept current on the passage of Tropical Storm Lisa. By 5 am, it seemed that she would pretty much spare the Cayman Islands, as she was veering north as she gained strength.

24.

To: Louis Bodden
From: Oren Goldberg
Re: Our Chat
Hi Louis,

I hope you get this. Wi-fi appears to be down in Frank Sound, but I'm attempting to send you this email from my phone.

I really do appreciate your wanting to help, but at this precise moment I cannot bear the thought of selling my father's lovely little hotel, then watching as it's pulled down and rebuilt. Even with another storm on the way. Quite frankly, I would rather go down with the ship (well not literally). So it's a no to your people.

OG
Oren Goldberg, MBE
President
The Corniche Hotel Trust Ltd.

There was nothing wrong with Lorna Paige Ebanks' looks. Nothing at all. Her own mother remarked on this one day after dropping a young Lorna to school on Walkers Road many, many moons ago. "Nice figure, good posture, pimples. She would be a real nice lookin' girl if only she could diet off that chip on her shoulder." As a girl Lorna was remarkably athletic and slim, and her mother had also once said she could have been a movie star.

"You got the same measurements as Audrey Hepburn," Mama had informed her, while driving her home from a meeting with the headmaster to discuss Lorna's attitude after an incident involving a groped breast and a male student's broken nose. "But much greener eyes."

Yet here she was, decades later, cleaning rooms for rich foreigners. While it was true that her eyes were greener, her mouth was also twice as big and her fists twice as likely to engage with anyone who crossed her.

Hurricanes always reminded Lorna of her mother, from whom she learned to prepare for storms and all of life's other contingencies. She had been abandoned by a worthless husband who refused to give them any support – Flinders Ebanks hadn't even bothered to move a full mile up the road when he left to cohabitate with his younger pregnant mistress. The new house was grand, sturdy and stormproof; built on higher ground at the end of a driveway with a real fence and double gates that could be closed at night. It would take Lorna and her mother years of loans, hard work and cinder blocks bought a few at a time to build the humble but comfortable cottage and terraced garden that stood on the large lot today. Her father had been happy to give them the land. He had wanted to remarry and the two-acre lot and cottage were inferior, so not suited to his new family and life. This was perhaps the one piece of good fortune that had ever come to her and her poor old mother. It meant she owned it all outright and it had suffered about as much damage as the Corniche.

"Poor Mama," escaped from Lorna's mouth before her tired mind could even stop her mouth from talking to the tired reflection that was staring back at her while she squeezed her mop into the drain. It was nearly as tired as her hands, which were raw from the morning's work. Her fingers were aching from grasping the mop and broom, and the skin on both palms was red and cracked from moisture and friction. The rest of her body was thankfully numb, but Lorna knew this wouldn't be the case by the time she could lower herself into bed and ease her tired but clean carcass in between her lovely white cotton sheets sometime late tonight.

"Did you say something?" asked Oren. She spun around. He hadn't been listening to her. While she stared to the south, he had been looking westward, out to sea and down at the beach. She shook her head and willed herself to focus on the job ahead.

"I know this is going to sound insane, but there's something quite beautiful about standing the middle of all this destruction. Does that sound crazy?" Oren was leaning over the railing of Penthouse 4 surveilling the island.

"I'm glad you said it first. It makes you realize just how small and insignificant we all are." Lorna was subdued, drained of adrenaline and impossible to excite

"If we was millennials we would have our phones out takin' pictures," added Lorna. There was damage. There was going to be damage and fallen power lines and flooding, but other than the conspicuous nudity of the trees, things along Seven Mile Beach didn't look so bad. It looked dramatically different from their vantage point, but Lorna was in agreement with Oren and Sharon.

"Have you ever seen anything like it?"

There was sand. Lots of it. Yes, granted this was a beach but Tropical Storm Lisa had somehow churned and deposited tons and tons of sand that was so white that it hurt the eyes and distributed it along the beach, dumping several truckloads at their back door.

Seven Mile Beach had been renewed. White sand was everywhere and it bolstered and extended the existing strip by an astonishing distance.

"Once before. Hurricane Allen. I was real young. Just about doubled the width o' Seven Mile Beach."

Still more white sand, almost whiter than any of them had ever seen, filled the swimming pool and had deposited a mammoth dune, effectively sealing the Corniche's double doors.

"Don't laugh at me, but do you remember that story in the Bible about manna from heaven?"

"We can't eat it, but we got plenty to work with here, I guess."

"Yeah. Bags of sand."

The Corniche was going to need a little work before they were ready to reopen its lovely old double doors. The lap pool was full of sand and there had been a few leaks and breeches.

"Sorry, Lorna. About yesterday, I mean."

"Oren, what the hell you would do without someplace to go every mornin'? Come to think of it, what would I do? What would we all do?"

"Sorry," he said again. "Just ignore my griping like you always do. Everything just got to be a little too much. It's been an overwhelming couple of weeks. And it's not even crazy season yet. You know?"

"I know, baby. I know better than most." It was a short comment and sentence, even for Lorna. But it did the trick. Once again the two friends were entirely sympatico once again

*

"Well if that was the big one for this decade, we can all rest easy." Oren once again leaned over the railing and surveyed their domain.

"You can say that twice. I only hope it doesn't mean the next one wipes us off the face of the beach."

"Who knows what the future holds. I'm just thankful we're still here. In business. All of us."

"This could have been so much worse. I mean, sure. There's damage, but everyone's accounted for."

"Everybody but one," said Bobby in a suspiciously smug voice.

"Who?"

"Apparently, there's one person missing."

"Who? Any idea? Anybody we know?" It was rare for someone to die in the storms. There was a long-standing tradition of safety thanks to Caymans' disaster preparedness and a building code that was envied throughout the region.

"According to the Marl Road and the police scanner and my cousin on the force, it's somebody we all know.

"Who? That's so sad..."

"You might not think so when you hear the gossip. The police are searching for a single white female. Regular visitor to the island for some years. One Ms Davis. Apparently her first name is Natasha. Did you know that?" Bobby looked smug as he shared the news.

"You're joking," said Lorna.

"Nope. Rental car by the side of the road in Bodden Town. Near the public beach, with a big tree branch forced clear through the windscreen by the force of the wind and out the rear. No foul play suspected as all her belongings were found on the passenger seat when the car was found. Wallet, cash, travel documents were all in an orange handbag. No news on the little gun, but I assume they found that too."

"Good," spat Lorna. "Dah wah yuh get. I hope Lisa blew that crook-woman clean off the face of this earth."

"I knew I should have punched out the bitch and taken that Birkin bag when I had the chance," said Sharon as she followed the lines of a slightly tousled but undamaged Seven Mile Beach to the South. "I'll never have another chance to own one."

"We'll all start dropping hints about orange Birkin bags around Hugh before Christmas. Problem solved," added Oren.

25.

"It's official! The staff and management at the Corniche hotel are happy to report that we have passed all of the relevant inspections and will be opened for business in the coming days. Please call our dedicated reservations hotline on 001-345-916-7747 to confirm your existing bookings."

They said their goodbyes in private before getting into Sharon's car. Sharon had promised herself that she would not get emotional seeing Hugh off. They drove in silence, only separating their hands when Sharon needed her left one to indicate turns. It would be six weeks before they could see each other again. Hugh was still amazed, not only by Sharon's planning but also with the part she had played in the execution in the disposal of Pratt's body.

"You mean you actually touched him? I don't know whether to be amazed or impressed that you had the fortitude to pick him up at one end and swing him over the bluff."

"Not just that. I wrapped him up, rolled him into plastic like a cigar and sealed the package at both ends with tape. Aren't you disgusted with what I've done?"

"I'm impressed as all hell. You've saved Miss Lorna from at the very least having to testify at an inquest. And the Corniche. You've saved the Corniche from all that bad press."

"No Hugh, you've saved the Corniche." Sharon still hadn't processed this aspect of Hugh's visit. With little more effort than it had taken to write and sign a cheque, Hugh had swooped in and become an investor and shareholder. She knew of incredible wealth all around her, and while the cars seemed to get more expensive and the price of everything from coffee to homes kept going up, she couldn't remember seeing such a grand gesture – in one stroke it had saved them all, along with their way of life and their little hotel on the beach.

"It wasn't entirely selfless. It looks like a sound enough investment and owning shares in a local institution will go a long way to help my case applying for a permanent residence."

Sharon didn't know what else to say. Yes, there was damage. There was going to be some destruction, as even the weakest of storm systems brought high winds and flooding. But Sharon could see as she made her way into town via the Esterly Tibbetts that there wasn't much wrong with Cayman that a few days of bright sunshine couldn't fix. And if there were two things that they would always have in surplus, it was sunshine and sunsets.

Sharon had been impressed by Hugh during the storm, too. There would be more outings in their future. They no longer had to spend all their time together alone and hidden from local eyes. With the purchase of the condo, their future communal home, they were eventually going to need to venture out in public together but it seemed better to find a way to have some control over their coming out than if the news was to hit the Marl Road and they got talked about like some delicious scandal. They could at least test the waters and gauge public opinion. She still had to come clean and break the news to her father, who she anticipated would voice some disapproval if not shame. But she was an adult and no longer his little girl. And this really wasn't something sordid.

The terminal was eerily empty. Some hotels were still scrambling to be ready for the tourists, both in the short and medium term. The usually hectic winter season would be delayed, but it would come eventually.

"Well I guess this is it," Sharon said hoarsely.

"Yes, but just for a few... I say, Sharon. Are those people waving at us?" The modern terminal building was mammoth compared to its first incarnation but by the standards of many other terminals it was still somewhat modest in its size, fittingly for the island and its architecture. It was commonplace in Cayman for departing passengers to greet those arriving and wish one another a bon voyage or a welcome home on the pavement. Sharon had got out of the car first to get the attention of a porter so that Hugh would not have to lift his own luggage.

"Oh, Jesus. Not today."

"What is it? Do you know them? Who are they?"

"It's my parents. I didn't even know they were arriving today."

"Just relax darling – they're your parents, you can give them a lift home."

"In the same car?"

"Now be nice."

"I don't have any choice. They're wheeling themselves and their booty right at us."

"Smile. We've said goodbye. I'm just going to leave casually."

"Oh God, Hugh. Don't leave like this. Maybe now is a good time. You think?"

"No. Tell them everything first. If they want to meet me, I'm happy for it to happen. But don't hit your father over the head with me. Goodbye, my darling."

Sharon smiled through clenched teeth as Mr and Mrs Phelan approached, wishing that she could be alone to cry in peace. Mrs Phelan was dressed to the nines but sporting glaring white new walking shoes and her father had paired his blazer with a baseball cap. Sharon was somewhat relieved that there was no political message on its front.

"Well, this is a surprise," said her mother, who Sharon noticed was wearing a similarly forced smile.

"And convenient," said her father, kissing her cheek. "You can drop us home. Damn taxis so expensive."

"You're sure the house is okay?" her mother asked again.

"What about Lorna? Her garden mash up bad?"

Sharon had been particularly touched by the parting of ways between Hugh and Lorna, as she watched them embrace the way friends who have known one another for decades do. Or perhaps family. Sharon wished that Lorna were here in the car with them now to help smooth over the next few minutes.

"Will I still get to see you now that you got your own house?"

"More often than ever I'm afraid," had been Hugh's answer as he kissed Lorna's cheek. "I don't know if I should say this as you've probably heard it too many times this week. But you are nothing short of a rose, Lorna. A rose cast in iron."

"Try so hush," was Lorna's typical reply, but those who knew her the best knew that that the compliment was deserved and she was trying to receive it as best she could.

"I known grown men and hardened criminals who couldn't have handled the sort of pressure I've witnessed here. I've known some important men to wet their pants when faced with a barrel of a gun. But you two..."

"All in a day's work, baby. All in a day's work, and anyone who calls me a rose just earned a seat at my table for ever."

Watching this made Sharon love Lorna and Hugh even more.

"Baby girl, who that you was dropping at the airport? Somebody you work with?" Thank God. Her father had given her this one. Sharon was nodding her head and about to answer him in the affirmative when her mother, who had suddenly leaned forward and placed her head in between the two front seats to hear, made her jump: "Miami is getting so expensive. There wasn't a bargain or deal to be found anywhere. The shopkeepers could smell us coming. And people? Not a minute's peace. Around every corner we ran into another Caymanian. And never anybody you'd be glad to see at home."

Sharon knew what her mother was doing. She was taking advantage of her father's poor short-term memory to change the subject before it progressed. But she suddenly realized it was time to bite the bullet.

"Well, Daddy. It's funny you should ask, and I'm glad I spotted you here because I can take the drive home to tell you something."

9 798223 763376